SHADOW OVER SAN MATEO

LAURAINE SNELLING

BETHANY HOUSE PUBLISHERS
MINNEAPOLIS, MINNESOTA 55438

Published by Bethany House Publishers
A Ministry of Bethany Fellowship International
11400 Hampshire Avenue South
Minneapolis, Minnesota 55438
www.bethanyhouse.com

Printed in the United States of America by
Bethany Press International, Minneapolis, Minnesota 55438

Library of Congress Cataloging-in-Publication Data

Snelling, Lauraine.
    Shadow over San Mateo / Lauraine Snelling.
        p. cm. — (Golden filly series ; bk. 6)
    Summary: As sixteen-year-old Tricia grieves over the death of
her father, she loses interest in horse racing and begins to question
the wisdom of God.
    [1. Horse racing—Fiction. 2. Death—Fiction. 3. Fathers and
daughters—Fiction. 4. Christian life—Fiction.]
I. Title. II. Series: Snelling, Lauraine. Golden filly series ; bk. 6.
PZ7.S677Sh   1993
[Fic]—dc20   92-43514
                                                      CIP
ISBN 1-55661-292-3   AC

To Carolyne Mozel's
fifth and sixth grade class of 1992–93.
What a super bunch of kids—top readers,
excellent writers, and just plain fun.

LAURAINE SNELLING is a full-time writer who has authored several published books, sold articles for a wide range of magazines, and written weekly features in local newspapers. She also teaches writing courses and trains people in speaking skills. She and her husband, Wayne, have two grown children and make their home in California.

Her lifelong love of horses began at age five with a pony named Polly and continued with Silver, Kit, Rowdy, and her daughter's horse Cimeron, which starred in her first children's book *Tragedy on the Toutle*.

CHAPTER 1

Just get through the ceremonies. Get through the ceremonies. Tricia Evanston hung on to her brother's words as the waves of applause rolled from the stands and across the track infield. Trish and her thoroughbred, Spitfire, had just won the famed Belmont Classic, the third diamond in the Triple Crown. Trish was the first woman jockey to win the honor.

But none of it mattered now. Not the trophies, not the applause, not the money. Unknown to her during the race, Trish's father had died at the hospital just before the race of her life began. When she didn't see him in the crowd, a nod from her brother confirmed her worst fears.

Just get through. Don't think. Don't feel. Get through.

Trish responded to the media as they clamored for her attention. She waved and smiled. And smiled some more. Her jaw felt like it would crack from the strain. Tears flowed freely down her cheeks.

She didn't dare look at her brother, David, and just leaned on the arm he had clamped around her. Spitfire stood at attention, ears forward, as the syndicate owners lined the shallow brick risers behind them. The blanket of white carnations covered the horse's withers and up onto his neck. When the cameras flashed again, he blew on Trish's neck, then nudged David.

Patrick O'Hearn, their trainer and friend, clenched Spitfire's reins with one hand and Trish's shoulder with the other. "Easy, lass," he whispered.

Trish could hear him murmuring. She bit her lip until the sticky-sweet taste of blood nearly made her gag. Patrick's voice had that same soothing song her father's had; the song that calmed horses and riders—and now broke her heart.

Trish brought her mind back to the moment through sheer force of will. Now they would go up for the trophies. The biggest, shiniest engraved bowl was for the winner's owner—Hal Evanston. Only he wasn't there. He would never be there again. Trish clamped her teeth tighter.

"I'll take him now, lass." Patrick loosened Trish's fingers from Spitfire's reins. He handed her the racing saddle and nodded toward the scales. As the trainer led the colt away, David and Hal's long-time friend Adam Finley gripped Trish's arms and led her to the scale.

Trish weighed in and then strode between the two men up the broad brick steps to the podium. Hands reached out to shake hers. "Thank you . . . yes, thank you." The words came stilted, mechanical.

"And now, ladies and gentlemen, the moment we've been waiting for . . ." John McKay, famous thoroughbred-racing announcer, shook her hand. ". . . Tricia Evanston, at sixteen, is not only the first female to win the Triple Crown, but the youngest ever to win it. You put on quite a show, young lady."

"Thank you," was all Trish could say.

"As you know, folks, this win is a family affair. Spitfire, bred and raised by Hal Evanston of Runnin' On

Farm, is now the official winner of this year's Belmont Cup . . ." He paused for a moment. ". . . accepted by his son, David Evanston." Trish could see the fleeting question on the man's face.

David stepped forward. "Thank you." He leaned into the microphone. "My father would be very proud of this honor. We all thank you." He raised the ornate silver Tiffany bowl in the air and smiled to the crowd.

Her teeth were clamped so tightly, it was almost impossible to smile, but Trish managed somehow. Just as McKay started to present her trophy, someone whispered in his ear.

Trish dashed the tears away. She *had* to be able to speak into the microphone—now!

"Ladies and gentlemen," McKay said, then paused. "I have an announcement to make." He paused again. A hush fell over the stands. "Ah-h-h . . ." He cleared his throat. The pain in his voice was obvious. "Fifteen minutes ago . . . about the time the horses broke from the gate . . . Hal Evanston died at the hospital. That is why . . . his son is here in his place to accept the trophy. Racing has lost a fine and generous man." He bowed his head, then looked to Trish and David. "Our hearts go out to you, Trish, David."

Sobs racked Trish's shoulders. She heard David blowing into his handkerchief. A baby wailed somewhere in the crowd. To honor Hal, the red-coated bugler stepped out onto the track and raised the long brass horn to his mouth. The clear notes of *Taps* lifted on the breeze and echoed across the infield to bounce back from the trees on the far side. The final notes seemed to hang on the air before fading away.

Trish stepped to the microphone. "We did it, Dad."

Her voice broke. She took a deep breath. "You—we—we won—the Triple Crown. I love you." She waved to the crowd, which broke out in thunderous applause. With David at one side and Adam on the other, Trish turned and left the podium area. Secret service men held back insensitive reporters as they shouted questions. Strobe lights flashed.

Trish concentrated on putting one foot in front of the other. *Down the stairs,* her mind prodded. *Follow the dirt back into the tunnel under the stands.* They turned left and exited through a door into the entrance area.

"There's a limo waiting outside," Trish heard someone say.

"Martha, you go with them, I'll take care of the questions," Adam said to his wife. He gave Trish and David a hug before he turned to the reporters.

Martha took his place, and with three men in front and more on each side, they passed through the crowd like the prow of a boat parting the sea; out the door and down the blue canopy-covered walk. Hanging baskets of geraniums passed in a pink blur.

Trish sank into the seat of the limo as though she were weighted down by the sorrow of the whole world. After the door slammed shut, she rubbed her face into David's shirt, and finally let the tears come. "He can't be gone, he can't." She thrashed from side to side, trying to wipe away the agony.

With her arms around her brother's chest, she could feel the heaving of his own sobs.

"I can't believe it, either," David cried into her hair.

Martha Finley handed them each a tissue, and rubbed Trish's back.

The limo slowed and stopped at the emergency entrance to the hospital.

Trish looked up. The windows blurred, and she wiped her eyes again. It was like looking through glass sheeted with rain. She leaned her head against the back of the seat and closed her eyes.

The man in the three-piece suit who had been sitting across from them passed her his handkerchief. Trish blew her nose and mopped her eyes—again. When she opened them, she saw her mother opening the side door.

"Oh, Mom!" Trish scrambled from the car and flung herself into Marge's arms. When David stepped out, the three clung together like lone survivors in a raging sea.

"I want to see Dad." Trish drew back. "I have to, Mom."

Marge nodded. With her arms around the waists of her children, she guided them to the second-floor room where Hal lay in the bed as if he were asleep. Trish had seen him like that many times before. Her mother had always said, "Go ahead, wake him. He wants you to." But this time, Trish knew there was no waking him.

She sank into a chair by the bed, and picked up her father's hand. She smoothed the back of it with her fingertips. "He looks so peaceful." Trish caught her breath, as if waiting for him to breathe. She felt her mother's hand on her shoulder and leaned her cheek against it.

"He's even smiling—sort of." The quiet of the room seeped into Trish, surrounded her. She laid Hal's hand back on the white blanket. "I love you, Dad," she whispered. "I love you." Her tears fell unchecked and soaked the sheet. Somewhere in the depths of her mind and heart, Trish heard her father's voice again, just as she'd heard it at the track: *I have fought the good fight, Tee. I have won my race. I love you.* "Oh, Dad, I need you."

Trish felt as if she were swimming in her own tears.

When she lifted her head, the heavy weight she'd felt in the limo washed over her again. She tried to stand but her legs were like rubber. David caught her before she crumpled. Trish leaned against him, and felt her mother support her other side. When Trish gained her footing, the three started toward the door. They turned together and with one voice said, "Goodbye."

In the hall, a woman waited with Martha Finley. She introduced herself. "I'm Chaplain Saunders. If you'd like, we can talk in the chapel. It's right this way."

Adam Finley met them halfway. He put his arm around Marge's shoulder. "Whatever we can do for you—"

Marge nodded. "We're going to the chapel now."

Trish's eyes and nose were still a fountain, but her mouth felt like a desert. She stopped for a drink of water.

The afternoon sun, streaming through a stained-glass window, bathed the chapel in soothing blues and greens. Trish still felt weak as she collapsed onto a padded chair. Martha Finley pressed a glass of water into her hand, and she smiled her thanks.

"N-now what?" Trish forced herself to straighten up in the chair and look at the chaplain.

"Your father's body will be taken to a funeral home and prepared for the flight to Portland. Someone will have to make the flight arrangements . . ."

"I will take care of that," Adam offered without hesitation.

"And you'll need to choose a casket . . ."

"I can help you with that," Martha volunteered.

Trish watched her mother collapse, weeping, into David's arms. No matter how much she wanted to, Trish didn't have the strength to reach them. She felt as if she were floating above them, watching all that went on. They couldn't be discussing her father, not *her* dad. Surely he was down at the barn, or at home, or—she felt a shudder that started at her toes and worked its way up to the top of her head. She huddled down in the chair, clamped her teeth again, this time to stop the shaking.

"Trish? Trish!" The voice seemed to come from far away.

She tried to take another sip of water, but the glass fell from her hands and bounced on the brown tweed carpet.

"Trish, put your head between your knees." She heard the voice and at the same time felt a hand pushing her head down. Then a blanket was gently wrapped around her shoulders.

All of a sudden Trish threw back the blanket and leaped to her feet. Marge started after her, but a nurse met Trish in the hall and after one look at her face steered her to a rest room. A cool hand supported Trish's head and a strong arm held her middle as she threw up into the toilet bowl.

When the worst was over the nurse handed her a wet washcloth. "Better now?" Trish nodded and wiped her face.

"I can't go back in there," she whispered. The tears started again.

"Come with me." An arm around Trish's shoulders, the nurse gently led her to an empty room with an open window, and held her while she cried.

"It's not fair," Trish heard herself saying.

"No, dear, it's not." The nurse brushed the damp hair from Trish's cheek. "Your father was a fine man. And he was so proud of you."

"You knew him?"

"Oh yes. Hal was a favorite around here, even for the short time he was with us. You know, nurses really appreciate a patient who is grateful for their help." She smoothed Trish's hair again. "Why, his faith just lit up the room. We all felt it every time we walked in there."

Trish looked up to see tears glistening in the nurse's eyes. "Yeah, he was like that." Trish bit her lip and sniffed. "I didn't get to say goodbye—or anything." She dropped her forehead to the nurse's shoulder. "I didn't want my dad to die."

"I know. None of us did." The nurse reached over and pulled tissues from a box.

Trish felt hot, then cold. *God, how can I live without him?* she thought.

"Trish?" David came into the room. "We're ready to go now, okay?"

Trish nodded, and squeezed the nurse's hand. "Thanks" was all she could manage.

Marge was talking with a doctor when David and Trish returned to the chapel.

"I can give you some sleeping pills, tranquilizers," the doctor was saying. "It might make these next hours easier."

Trish shrugged and shook her head when the doctor looked at her. "They can't bring my father back."

"No, thank you," Marge said softly. "We'll be all right." She took the arms of her children and stepped into the hall.

Reporters were swarming around the door outside. "What will be done with Spitfire? Is he finished racing?"

Adam Finley spoke for the others. "Spitfire will be

shipped to BlueMist Farms in Kentucky as soon as possible. That's all I can tell you now."

As that announcement crashed into her consciousness, Trish felt the last shred of hope being torn away.

CHAPTER 2

"Trish, you knew Spitfire was going to Kentucky," David whispered in her ear.

"I know." Trish climbed into the limo and huddled next to her mother. She wrapped both arms around herself to try to stop the shaking.

"Just a minute." Adam stepped back out of the car and spoke with one of the secret service men. The man left and within a few minutes returned with several hospital blankets. Marge took them and gratefully wrapped two around her daughter.

A gray fog stole into Trish's head. As the warmth of the blankets and her mother's arms cradled her limp body, she felt herself floating again. When they reached the hotel, Trish barely felt the carpet beneath her feet as Adam Finley helped her to the room. Martha spoke softly while she helped her with her boots and silks.

Trish forced her eyes open when she heard her mother's voice. "Sleep, Tee. Jesus loves you, and so do I."

Trish barely nodded. "Me too, Mom." She wanted to ask a question but the fog hung too thick.

A raging thirst woke Trish hours later. When she tried to stand, the room whirled and she sat down again. She fumbled with the switch on the bedside lamp. The wings of the wood-carved eagle glistened in the soft light on her nightstand. The figure had been her gift to her father for Christmas, to remind him of the promise of the Father bearing him up on eagles' wings. The sight of it was too much, and Trish shoved it onto a shelf at the back of the closet.

Reaching the bathroom, she grabbed a bunch of toilet paper and wiped her eyes again and blew her nose. If only her father were asleep in the next room. Pretending didn't work.

She chug-a-lugged a glass of water, then refilled it to take with her.

Noticing a light coming from the living room, Trish opened the door. Martha Finley sat knitting in a wing chair, her feet propped up on a hassock. Adam was asleep on the sofa, snoring softly.

"Oh, Trish, can I get you anything? A glass of orange juice, or something to eat?" The lamp cast a halo around the older woman's white hair.

"Where's Mom?"

"She's sleeping, I think. So is David. We'll be going to our room in a bit. I just wanted to be here in case you needed anything."

"Thanks. I'm okay." Trish thought her own voice sounded like a frog. Back in her room, she switched off the light and was asleep almost before her head hit the pillow.

———

Trish felt herself smiling before she opened her eyes the next morning. How incredibly wonderful . . . She and Spitfire had won the Belmont Stakes, the final jewel in the Triple Crown! Then the awful reality struck . . . Her father was *dead*.

Trish rolled over and smothered her cries in the pillow. "It's not fair!" She punched the pillow with her fists. Would her broken heart ever mend?

This can't be real; it's like a nightmare. The words echoed through her mind. She squeezed her eyes shut. *If only it were just a bad dream.*

She sat bolt-upright in bed. *Dad always said God was his strength—our strength. But we prayed. Why didn't you answer, God?* She leaped from the bed and jerked on her clothes. She didn't want to think about it anymore.

"That's it! No more crying!" she ordered the swollen and blotchy face she saw in the bathroom mirror. She held a cold wet washcloth to her eyes for a minute, but it didn't help the puffy eyelids. She sniffed again and swallowed hard. "No more!"

By the time Trish had unbraided, brushed, and rebraided her dark wavy hair, she felt she had her armor in place. She squeezed toothpaste onto the brush and methodically brushed her teeth. Maybe doing all the routines would get her back on track, but when she looked in the mirror again she nearly lost it.

"Trish?" Her mother knocked on the bathroom door. "Are you all right?"

"Uh . . . yeah, I'm okay." She opened the bathroom door, but couldn't face her mother. "I gotta go, Mom. I need to feed Spitfire—work him and stuff, you know. See you later." She ducked her head and bolted for the door.

At the car, she dug in her pockets. No keys. She couldn't go back up there. Feeling the weight of the entire planet on her shoulders, she leaned her forehead on the rim of the car roof.

"I'll drive," David said from behind her. He nudged her over so he could insert the key in the lock.

Trish felt like shoving him back, but what good would it do? She stomped around to the passenger's side and climbed in.

"Quit acting like a spoiled brat," David said in his most reasonable big-brother tone.

Trish stared at him. *How could you. . . ?* She bit her lip and tried not to let the dam burst again. *What are we doing? We never act like this.*

"Look, I know you're mad at God . . . and all the world." David's voice cracked. "Well, so am I." Trish could hardly hear him. He took a deep breath. "Let's just get through this day, Trish. Can we do that?"

No tears! her mind screamed. "Whatever." She stared straight ahead and wished she didn't have to get through this day or any other day.

The guard at the gate nodded them through. His usual smiling face was somber. When David parked by their barn, he leaned his forehead on his crossed hands on the steering wheel. After a bit he straightened and turned toward Trish. His eyes filled with tears. "I just can't believe it. I can't believe he's gone."

Trish clamped down on her lip again. She gritted her teeth and swallowed hard. "Yeah, I know." She opened the car door and leaped out. When she tried to whistle to Spitfire nothing came. *You can't whistle when you're drowning in tears.* The little voice inside she called Nagger seemed to chuckle with glee. It always seemed happiest when she was in trouble.

As she entered the long green and white barn, a reporter peeled himself off the wall and approached her. "Can I ask you a few questions, Trish? I know this is a terrible time for you, so I'll keep it short."

Trish stared at him, shock paralyzing her vocal cords.

Had he lost his mind? How could she talk to anyone now?

He took her silence for agreement. "Do you know when the funeral will be?" Trish shook her head. "What will you do with Spitfire?" Trish shook her head again and pushed past him. "Will he go directly to stud? How about the Breeder's Cup? You said once you'd like to race him there . . ."

"Get on with you now." Patrick shook a gnarled fist in the man's face. "I already answered all your questions. You be leaving the kids alone."

"Just doing my job." The man touched a finger to his forehead in a salute. "Trish?" He raised his voice. "I want you to know how sorry I am. Please accept my condolences. Your father was one in a million. We'll all miss him . . ."

Trish buried her face in Spitfire's mane. *Be polite.* Nagger seemed to perch right on her shoulder.

"Thank you." She heard David's voice outside the stall. "We'll let you know what's going to happen with Spitfire as soon as we know ourselves."

"Okay, lass, let's get the old man saddled here so you can walk him nice and easy. He's got an awful lot of pep for running a mile and a half yesterday." Patrick handed Trish the bridle, then spread the saddle cloth and settled the saddle in place.

Trish slipped the headstall over Spitfire's nose, then ears; buckled the chin strap, all in one easy, fluid motion. She didn't need her mind in gear to perform these tasks. Spitfire blew gently in her face and lipped a strand of her bangs. She stared into his eyes. No mischief lurked there this morning, only a gentle caring.

Trish rubbed up behind the horse's ears and underneath the headstall. "You're such a good fella," she whispered.

"They sense things." Patrick checked the girth again. "I don't know how, but horses—most animals, seem to know when something bad has happened. He's trying to tell you how much he cares, how much he loves you."

Trish nodded, and raised her knee to be boosted into the saddle. She didn't dare look at Patrick; the kindness in his voice was enough. *You will not cry again!* she commanded herself.

David snapped the lead shank in place and handed Trish her helmet. "Come on, fella." He stopped at the end of the barn. "Would you rather just walk him around in the barn here? A couple of turns would loosen him up. That's why the aisles are so wide, you know."

"I know." Trish gathered up her reins. "But I think being outside will be better. Maybe the wind will blow away some of my fuzziness."

"Hey, wait up."

Trish turned to look over her shoulder. Red Holleran, the young jockey she'd dated in Kentucky, jogged up the sandy stretch. She would recognize his red hair anywhere. Had he been around yesterday after the race? Trish couldn't be sure. The evening was a blur in her mind.

"Hi." He reached up to clasp her hand. "You okay?"

Trish ducked her head in a kind of nod. *If okay means I'm here and riding, yes, it fits. But how will I ever be really okay again?*

"I'm so sorry, Tee."

Trish squeezed Red's hand. "Yeah, me too." She looked beyond Spitfire's twitching ears. Out there all the world seemed so normal. People were laughing, someone was singing, and the cicadas were warming up for their daily concert from the elm trees. Spitfire took a deep breath and exhaled noisily.

"I could work the filly for you, if you'd like."

"That's okay," David answered for Trish. "Why don't you walk over with us. Then we can come back for Sarah's Pride while Trish is walking Spitfire."

"Sure. Or does Patrick need some help?"

Trish felt a warm spot in her middle. Red really cared, she could tell. She squeezed his hand again. All the way out to the track, her hand stayed warm.

Spitfire jogged sideways as soon as David released the lead. Ears forward, neck arched, he danced in place, then set out at an easy extended walk. Trish let her feet dangle below the iron stirrups. It would be so easy to let her mind wander, but even in her fuzzy state she knew better. That's the way accidents happened.

Later Trish realized she had spoken with people and gone through all the proper motions, even talking with a reporter who evaded the barriers put up by Patrick, David, and Red. But life seemed to be happening at the end of a long tunnel or the small end of a telescope. If she kept it all far enough away, she didn't hurt so much.

The meeting with Spitfire's syndicate owners was held back at the hotel about noon. Trish nodded and answered in all the right places. When the Shipsons discussed the barn and accommodations for Spitfire at BlueMist Farms, Trish agreed that everything sounded great. When Adam Finley talked about the horse van he'd reserved for the trip back to Kentucky, Trish nodded again. A van was a van, and even though they'd had an accident with one coming up on the New Jersey Turnpike, it wouldn't happen again, she was sure.

But inside Trish screamed *No! Let me take him home. I want Spitfire at Runnin' On Farm where he belongs. I need him there. He needs me. No one else can even ride him! Please, please, let me—* But just like keeping Sarah's Pride under control, Trish rode herself with a tight rein.

Even when Adam talked about the flight arrangements to take the family and Hal's body back to Vancouver, Trish stared straight ahead. She clenched her teeth to shut off the voices in her head. *Just get through this. Just get through.* She repeated the phrase again and again until it assumed its own beat, like a bass drum in a parade. *Just get through.*

But when Martha Finley reached over and took her hand, Trish almost lost control. She could feel the tears burn behind her eyes. She sniffed and took her hand back. *Just get through.*

"Are you coming, Tee?" Her mother laid a hand on Trish's shoulder.

"Uh—where?" Trish tried to shut off the inner cadence so she could answer.

"To the funeral home. We're going to pick out the casket."

Trish forced her legs to lift her body off the chair. How long had she been sitting there? She looked around the room. "Where's everyone?"

"They left a bit ago. Do you want some lunch first?"

Trish shook her head. "No, let's get it over with."

"You don't have to go if you don't want to." Marge put both hands on Trish's shoulders.

Trish really looked at her mother. Marge seemed to have lost weight; her face was pale and drawn. There were deep creases from her nose to the sides of her mouth. Did they all look like that? "I'll go."

On the drive over, Trish pulled herself back to the small end of the telescope. The woman at the funeral home spoke so softly Trish could hardly hear her. *Oh well, do I really want to hear her?*

They entered a large room that displayed a wide variety of caskets—blue, gray, brown, wood tones, metallic, burnished. *Just get through*. Trish felt like heaving. They couldn't put her father in a box like this. Not her father. He was so alive and real.

He's not alive anymore. Trish dug her fingernails into her fists.

"Don't you have a simple wooden box?" Marge asked. "That's what Hal wanted."

"Are you sure?" David looked at his mother, confusion written on his face.

"Yes, he and I—uh—we discussed these things a long time ago. I have all his suggestions, requests. He wanted to make it as easy for us as possible."

"You know . . ." The woman paused. "Yes, we do have some wooden caskets." She led them to another part of the room. There were several of plain wood. One had a cross burned in the cover.

"I'll take that one," Marge said firmly. After writing the check, she thanked the woman for her help, and they stepped out into the entryway where Adam and Martha were waiting for them.

"They'll have everything ready and at JFK Airport by 12:30," Adam said. "I talked with the director while you were downstairs. He assured me that there would be no difficulties."

"Thank you." David nodded as he reached to shake Adam's hand. Instead, the older man drew the younger into a hug.

Just get through. Trish slipped behind her mother. She could manage as long as no one touched her.

That night Trish was already in bed when Marge came in to talk with her. She sat down on the edge of the bed. "Is there any way I can help you, Tee?"

Trish shook her head. At least when she was asleep, she didn't have to think.

Marge reached over and smoothed a lock of hair behind her daughter's ear. Trish flinched.

"It'll be easier for all of us if we help each other. You know your dad wanted it that way." Marge waited. The silence stretched, broken only by a car horn honking on the street. "I know you're trying to tough this out, but crying does make things easier."

Trish could hear the tears in her mother's voice. She didn't dare look for fear her own would break through.

Marge reached for a tissue. "Where's the eagle?"

"I put it away."

"Where?"

"In the closet." Trish felt Marge get up from the bed, then heard the closet door slide open. The eagle was on the top shelf. She knew her mother had picked it up. If she let herself, Trish could picture the light glinting off the intricately carved wings, but she pushed the image from her mind.

Marge sighed.

As her mother reached the door, Trish turned over and asked the question that had been plaguing her. "How come he died—right then, I mean."

"It was a massive hemorrhage in his lungs. The doctors tried . . . nothing helped. We were on our way out the door—to come to the track . . ." Marge paused and blew her nose. "Just like that, he was gone."

Trish didn't answer. She couldn't. One tear squeezed out from between her clenched eyelids and slipped down her cheek.

CHAPTER 3

Trish woke feeling as if the world were crumbling around her. Today they would fly back to Portland. Homecoming was supposed to be a celebration. She and her best friend since kindergarten, Rhonda Seabolt, had talked about a huge party. There wouldn't be one now.

Trish forced herself to get up. No matter what, Spitfire needed to be worked. *Why?* Her little voice spoke softly for a change. *He won't be running again.*

"Just because," Trish muttered as she crammed her feet into her boots. "And Sarah's Pride will be running again. She needs lots of work."

David met her at the door. "You all packed?"

Trish shook her head. "I suppose you are."

"Yeah, I couldn't sleep."

Trish looked closely at her brother's face. He had the same look she'd seen in her own mirror. While David tried to be strong for her, she knew he was hurting, too.

At least the reporters had backed off. Trish found herself watching for them so she could run the other way. She also caught herself looking for a certain red-headed young man.

"Lookin' for anyone in particular?" Patrick grabbed for his hat as Spitfire tried to flip it off.

Trish could feel her neck get warm at Patrick's teas-

27

ing. "Come on, horse, let's get going here. Quit goofing around."

Spitfire rubbed his forehead against Trish's chest, nearly knocking her over. When she ignored his plea he blew grain saliva in her face.

"Okay, okay. I get the hint." Trish scratched under his headstall and along the top of his neck under his mane. When she turned to a familiar voice at the door, the colt draped his head across her shoulder, his favorite position.

"You want me to work Sarah's Pride so you can get done quicker?" Red asked.

"No, that's okay." Trish could feel her face getting warm again. Would she *never* quit blushing when Red was around? "What I mean is—" She looked to David for help. He'd disappeared. She could hear him talking to the filly in the next stall. "I mean, ahhh . . . thanks. We'd appreciate that."

Red seemed to sense her unwillingness to talk as he rode beside her around the track. Sarah's Pride kept him pretty busy. She still fought her rider, always wanting to run when another horse came by.

"Keep your mind on what you're doing," Red ordered the fractious filly as he pulled her down to a walk again. "You just can't seem to understand *jog*, can you?" The horse shook its head.

Trish felt a small grin turn up the corners of her mouth. If only they could ride like this forever. Their return to the barn came much too quickly.

"I'll see you on Friday night then?" Trish studied her boot rather than look Patrick in the face.

"How about Saturday morning? You'll be gettin' in too late to make a stop by here."

"Yeah, I keep forgetting the time change." She drew circles in the sand with her boot. "Ahhh, take good care of him, okay?"

Patrick nodded. "You needn't worry. Red here will work the girl, and Spitfire and I can walk for miles round and round."

"Come on, Trish," David interrupted. "We gotta get going."

Trish rubbed Spitfire's nose one more time. "See ya, fella." The colt nickered as she followed David down the aisle. Red fell into step beside her. He took her hand and squeezed it.

Their footsteps lagged.

"I'll still be here when you get back, you know."

"Really? I thought maybe Patrick was making that up." Trish felt a little flutter of what could only be called joy. "I thought—I hoped—I, uh, thought I'd see you in Kentucky at least."

"I'm riding back in your van, if that's okay with you."

"Okay? That's great. But aren't you missing out on a lot of mounts?"

Red shrugged. "There'll be others. Being with you is more important right now."

Trish felt the now familiar burning behind her eyes. "Thanks." The word croaked around the lump stuck in her throat.

David already had the car running when they caught up to him.

"See you Saturday then?" Trish chewed her lip.

When Red put both arms around her, Trish leaned against him. "I wish I could help you, Tee." His breath stirred the wisps of hair around her ear.

Trish couldn't answer. The lump was still there. *What*

can I say, anyway? No one can help. She wrapped both arms around his waist in answer. Her internal drum started thumping again. *Just get through*.

Red lifted her chin with one finger so his lips could find hers. The kiss was gentle, soft.

Trish pulled away. "Sorry." She swallowed other words she wanted to say. *Please understand*. How could she tell Red that she couldn't handle nice-and-gentle right now? Not and get through. Instead, she squeezed his hand and turned to fumble with the door handle of the car.

With one hand on her shoulder as if to hold her to him, Red opened the door with his right. Trish felt a second kiss on her ear as she slipped into the car.

"Take care now." Red gently closed the car door and thumped on the glass.

As they drove away, Trish forced herself not to look back. Even so, one tear sneaked by her control and slid down her cheek. She felt David's gaze when he stopped for a red light. But instead of answering his unspoken question, she huddled tighter in the corner. So many goodbyes.

Trish worked her way back to the small end of the telescope as she packed her suitcase. When she cleaned off the closet shelf, she saw that the eagle was gone.

"Mom . . ." She started to ask what happened to it, but stopped herself. *Who cares? It's just a wooden bird*.

———

Trish slept most of the flight home, mumbling a refusal when the flight attendant asked her food preference. She vaguely heard her mother do the same. Thanks to a half-full flight, Trish was able to lie down.

"Approaching Portland International." The pilot's voice worked like an alarm.

Trish sat up, clutching the gray blanket around her shoulders. David had stretched out, too, and was still asleep.

"Have we passed Mount Hood?" Trish asked. She felt too groggy to crawl over to the window seat to look out.

Marge raised her head from her hand and nodded. Trish could tell she'd been crying again. Pain for her mother briefly replaced her own. How would any of them manage without her father? She closed her mind against the thought of the days, months, and years ahead.

When the seat belt light went off, Trish pulled one bag from under the seat and waited for David to retrieve another from the overhead bins. Adam and Martha Finley led the way off the plane.

Staggering up the ramp, Trish caught a glimpse of Rhonda. Brad Williams, the other member of the four musketeers, was right behind her. *Their faces must mirror my own*, she thought. Sad, afraid to smile. For her it was the fear she'd never smile again.

"Oh, Trish," Rhonda whispered as she hugged her friend. "I can't believe this has really happened. Are you okay?" Rhonda wiped her tears away with the heels of her hands. "I can't seem to quit crying."

Trish just nodded as she felt her friends' arms wrap around her. Brad had included David in the community hug. *What's to say? What does okay mean anymore?* She felt the tears coming, and pulled away. Closeness to anyone always brought the tears on. And if she started crying, she was afraid she'd never stop.

"Please, I . . ."

Rhonda studied Trish's face and nodded. They were the kind of friends who didn't need to finish sentences.

The pain hit Trish afresh. Theirs was like the relationship she'd had with her father. He'd been able to read her mind, too. Was everything going to remind her of him? She felt as if she were running through a maze with no way out.

Brad slung Trish's pack over his shoulder and Rhonda picked up Trish's sports bag. She dropped it again to blow her nose.

"Come on," Brad said to Trish. "The van's in the short-term lot. David, if you want to head down for the rest of your luggage, we'll bring the van around. You coming, Tee?"

Trish turned to her mother and the Finleys. Marge nodded. "Adam, Martha, meet Brad Williams and Rhonda Seaboldt. They're like our own kids." Turning to the young people, she said, "Kids, I know you've heard of the Finleys. They've helped us beyond measure."

Adam shook Brad's hand. "Glad to meet you. We'll pick up our car, then, and follow you."

Trish watched as if from the other end of her telescope. It all seemed so pointless. She followed her friends, not really joining in on the conversation but making the right responses. Still, the drive from the parking lot to the baggage claim was silent. Trish stared out the window. It had started to rain. *How appropriate.*

———

Trish kept her distance for the next two days. The funeral would be on Thursday. The only time it seemed bearable was when she was down at the barn. Her nearly year-old filly, Miss Tee, took some time to adjust to Trish's return.

"You've grown so much." Trish stroked the little filly's ears. "You're not really a baby anymore." She smoothed the golden mane that was turning from brush to full length. Miss Tee sniffed Trish's hair and nibbled at her fingers. Trish dug in her pocket for another carrot. "Here; all you want are treats. We're gonna have to start working with you pretty soon. Has Brad been leading you around?" The filly shook her head and sniffed for another carrot.

Trish rubbed the tender spot between the filly's ears. She leaned on the fence and watched four-month-old Double Diamond race across the field. At the filly's snort, Trish released the halter and smiled as her namesake dashed after the colt and kicked up her heels. They really looked good, both of them. It seemed as if she'd been away from home for years, not intermittent weeks. She'd been gone most of May and half of June.

When Trish wandered out in the field where the racing stock pastured, she nearly lost it with old gray Dan'l. He trotted up as soon as she whistled, nickering his welcome and rubbing his forehead on her chest. He'd been her track tutor for the last few years, hers and most of the young stock. They used the old race horse to help train the new racers. He always set a calm example on the three-quarter-mile track at the farm and in the starting gates.

Trish scratched his cheek and fed him another carrot. At least with the horses she didn't have to try to talk. Even with all the guests coming and going, the house seemed empty. If only she could pretend that her father was at the hospital as he'd been for those weeks last fall.

But it was easier not to think about him at all. Not to look for him in the next stall. Not to remember his funny whistle as he worked with the horses. Not to—she fiercely shut her mind down again. It was like slamming a heavy truck door, one that had to stay shut.

Rhonda and Brad dropped by after school. Trish levered herself off her bed and dogtailed Rhonda back to the kitchen where Martha Finley had baked chocolate chip cookies. The four teenagers took theirs back into the living room where Adam had a fire going to chase the chill of a drizzly, windy afternoon.

"It's my California blood," he said, warming his backside in front of the blaze. "I don't do well in this dampness."

Trish crumbled her cookie and stared into the leaping flames. Talking took too much effort.

"We miss you at school," Rhonda ventured.

"Mmmm."

"*I* miss you."

Trish turned her head to look at Rhonda. "Me, too."

"You coming back for finals?"

"I guess."

Brad and Rhonda left soon after that. They and their families would join everyone at church for the memorial service.

That evening, Trish heard her mother on the phone with her grandparents in Florida.

"Why don't you come out later this summer, instead?" Marge said. "Then we can really have some time together. You know how I feel about traveling long distances to attend funerals."

Marge listened for a while. "But, Mother . . . No, please, stay there and come when Daddy is feeling better.

Yes, I'll call you soon. No, I'm as good as can be expected, I guess. God will get me through this. I can sense Him taking care of all of us."

Trish snorted and shook her head. She wanted to shake her mother. God was taking care of them? Right!

Wednesday afternoon, Pastor Mort found Trish down in the barn cleaning tack. Everything had gotten dusty while they'd been gone, so she set to work. It helped when there was something to do. The only other way to forget was to sleep. Pastor Mort sat down beside her on a bale of straw.

Trish greeted him with a nod, and kept on rubbing the saddle seat. She scrubbed her rag in the can of saddle soap and began another circle.

"I'll get right to the point, Trish. It would help if you would talk about both your father *and* your feelings. Your mother says you've pretty much walled yourself away from everyone."

Trish didn't flinch, her eyes riveted on the saddle. Her hand trembled a bit as she turned the leather to work on the other side. The silence between the two deepened, stretching like a rubber band pulled taut and about to snap.

Then Pastor Mort picked up a rag and dipped it in the saddle soap. He started on the bridle on the floor between them, rubbing the leather in smooth strokes.

Trish looked at him in surprise.

He smiled. "I had horses when I was young. You never forget how to clean tack." The rubber band relaxed.

Trish felt her shoulders slump. She hadn't realized how tense she was. If he didn't leave soon . . . She bit her lip till the pain forced back the tears.

"Trish, I know how much you hurt inside. You and

your dad had a really special relationship. Anyone could see that. And I know you must be so angry you want to tear things up." His voice floated through the telescope, encouraging Trish to close up the distance and talk with him.

"That's one of the problems with our society. We never allow people to grieve. I know you've all been grieving for a long time—a prolonged illness causes that in a family. Now you feel like God has let you down entirely; am I right?"

"He did!" The words exploded from the deep canyon of Trish's heart. She clamped her teeth on her lip, knowing if she said any more she'd fly apart into a million pieces and no one would ever be able to put her back together.

"It may seem that way, Trish. And I don't have any easy answers for you either. All I can say is that in spite of what we think and feel, God is in control. He loves us more than we can imagine, and promises to get us through times just like this."

Trish glared at the bald spot on the man's head as he bent over to smear more soap on his rag. *Another one of His promises? God doesn't live up to His promises*, she wanted to scream. "My dad said something like . . ." The pain tore into her subconscious mind and clamped off her words. She could not think about her dad, all the things he had said and taught her.

She took a deep breath, but thought she would choke on the lump in her throat. "Whatever . . ." she croaked, and the fury she felt was stuffed down further than ever.

———

The next day, Trish awoke promising herself she

would not cry at the funeral. That was after she'd punched and turned her damp pillow a few times. The tears she dammed up during the day spilled over at night.

She spent as much time as she dared down with the horses. David finally came and got her. "You're going to be late."

Trish glared at him. Swallowing her *Who cares?* she followed him back to the house. After jerking a brush through her hair and changing clothes, she joined her mother and the Finleys as they walked silently out to the waiting cars.

The silence enfolded Trish as she huddled in the backseat. *Sixteen-year-old kids shouldn't have to go to their father's funeral.*

CHAPTER 4

Nightmares are hobbyhorses compared to this.

Cars filled the church parking lot and down the streets. Trish watched people walk up the front steps of the church from the safety of her backseat. Her mother and David had already gone inside. *Come on, you can't just hide out here. You have to go in.* Her little Nagger was beginning to sound desperate.

Trish bit at her lip again. Why did inflicting pain on herself seem to help? She rolled down the window to let in some fresh air. The glass had steamed up. Breathing in the cold, damp air didn't help. Nothing seemed to help.

Get out, you chicken! she told herself in no uncertain terms. *You managed to get to the hospital; you can walk yourself inside the church. You'll get through this. You have to.* The sight of David coming out the side door of the cedar-sided building and striding purposefully toward the car was all the force she needed.

She stepped out quickly, shut the car door behind her, and followed her brother inside. Organ music swelled and filled the church. It reminded Trish of the family conference Pastor Mort had with them the night before. He said the service would be a celebration. Hal had wanted it that way.

In fact, Hal had planned the entire service—another reason Trish didn't want to be there. Her father had made a list of his favorite hymns and Bible verses. He'd asked that there be few flowers, preferring memorials to the jockey fund. He wanted everyone to remember and rejoice that he'd gone home. His race was finished.

But Trish couldn't rejoice. She stood behind her mother as Marge greeted the last of the families that had come to remember Hal.

Then she joined her family and the Finleys in the front pew. Rhonda was right behind her and squeezed Trish's shoulder. "You okay?" her eyes asked around the tears. Trish shook her head. She'd never be okay again.

———

That evening, Trish couldn't have told anyone about the funeral. She'd literally checked out. Her body was present, but not her mind. Her lip was raw and red, her head pounded, and her eyes burned from unshed tears. But she'd *gotten through*.

Long before dark, Marge offered Trish a pain pill and a sleeping pill. She took them without a second thought, and climbed into bed exhausted. Falling asleep was like tumbling down a long, dark tunnel. At the end she felt nothing.

Trish awoke early Friday morning. Her mouth felt like cotton balls and her head still pounded. Her eyes wouldn't focus. Everything looked about as blurry as she felt. She staggered to the bathroom, guzzled a glass of water, and stumbled back into bed—back down the tunnel to oblivion.

It seemed only moments later when she heard her mother calling her name, felt her mother's hand on her shoulder. "Trish, Trish. You need to get ready for your flight. The plane to New York leaves in an hour and a half. I let you sleep as long as I dared."

Trish rubbed the sleep from her eyes and pushed herself into a sitting position. She crossed her legs and held her head. It still throbbed, but not as bad as last night.

"Are you sure you're up to this?" Marge sat down on the edge of the bed and brushed a lock of hair from Trish's cheek. She tilted her daughter's chin with one finger so she could look into her eyes. "You know, you don't have to be superwoman. You could stay here and let David go."

Trish shook her head. "No. Every time they've tried moving Spitfire without me, there's trouble." She swallowed, but her throat was so dry it hurt. "Could you please get me a glass of water? I feel . . ." She shook her head. *Lousy, rotten, the pits*— None of those began to describe how she really felt. *Miserable, sick, lost.* The hole was too black and too deep to describe.

Marge patted Trish's knee. "I'll be right back."

Trish gulped the water down and asked for more. This time she forced herself out of bed and began pulling clothes out of the drawers to throw into her bag. She would only be gone three days—she didn't need much.

"You get a shower so you can navigate—I'll pack that." Marge handed her daughter the second glass of water. Trish sipped as she stared around the room. *Where are my boots?*

As she studied the room, her glance fell on the Bible verses pinned to the wall. Most of the three-by-five cards were in her father's handwriting. She looked away quickly. *Yeah, right.* The thoughts snarled like caged tigers in her mind. *Dad believed all those promises and what did it get him?* She kept her gaze straight ahead, and stomped to the bathroom. The only way was to keep those thoughts at the other end of the telescope. She was getting pretty good at that.

But even the sound of the shower failed to drown out a voice that whispered, *He got heaven. That's the point.* Trish gritted her teeth. Back in her room, she ripped the cards off the wall and dumped them in the wastebasket, careful not to read any of the words.

———

"Be careful." Marge hugged her daughter just before she and Adam Finley boarded the plane at Portland International Airport.

Trish nodded. She forced herself to return the hug. That old burning started in the back of her throat. If only everyone would leave her alone. No talking, no touching. She made the mistake of looking into her mother's tear-filled eyes.

"I—" Trish swallowed—hard. She had to. The burning had turned to fire that made her eyes water. "We'll call you tonight. Now, don't worry. You know we'll be all right."

She heard her mother's "God keep you," then slammed the telescope to full length. *Sure, just like He kept Dad, right?* She snorted in disgust.

Adam wisely refrained from commenting on the thunderclouds that furrowed Trish's brow. He just handed their tickets to the young man at the gate and walked down the ramp beside her.

As soon as they were airborne, Trish flipped her seat back and curled under the blanket. This time the plane was full so she couldn't stretch out. It didn't matter. She slipped back into that blessed long black tunnel where pain and sorrow didn't exist.

Adam woke her when the plane began its approach to John F. Kennedy Airport on Long Island. *How come I always wake up with a raging thirst?* This time she'd have to wait until they landed before she could get a drink of water.

"You okay?" Adam asked.

Trish nodded. She snapped her seat upright at the request of the flight attendant. Getting oriented sounded simple, but her brain refused to function. She didn't just need a drink of water, she needed a bucket of water poured over her head.

By the time they arrived at the car rental office, Trish was getting impatient to see Spitfire. How could people be so slow? Getting a car in New York took longer than anywhere else she'd ever been. She took a long drink of the Diet Coke she'd bought at the first snack bar. Would the line *ever* move? She wasn't the only one getting frustrated. Two businessmen behind them expressed their sentiments in language that fit the situation.

When they finally got the car, the traffic on the Beltway crawled along like a vast ribbon of parking lot. Trish slumped in her seat.

"It's too late to go to the track tonight." Adam glanced at his watch. "We'd be better off just checking in to the hotel and getting something to eat."

"I really wanted to see Spitfire first." Trish couldn't help voicing her desire.

"I know. We're still on Pacific time, but it's later here. Can you wait till morning?" Trish nodded. Nothing ever seemed to go right anymore. "You hungry?"

"I don't think so." She did a body check. Food just didn't seem necessary.

"You didn't eat on the plane." Adam tapped his brakes again when the taillights in front of them flashed red.

"I know." *Will this drive never end?* Trish knew she was being rude, but she couldn't seem to think of anything to say. It was easier to retreat to the other end of her telescope.

By the time she fell onto her hotel bed, the pounding headache had returned. She dug in her case for some pain pills and slugged two of them down. The face in the mirror seemed to have lost all life and color. The circles under her eyes were getting blacker. She poured a glass of water to leave on the nightstand and flicked off the light. If only it were that easy to flick off all that had happened.

———

In the morning, Trish braided her hair and brushed her teeth without looking in the mirror. Who needed reminders of how bad she looked?

"The horse van will be ready at 7:00," Adam said when he knocked on her door. "I'm checking out now. I'll meet you downstairs."

"Okay." Trish finished stuffing her things into the bag and checked the bathroom again. She switched off the lights as she left the room.

The sun was just pinking the eastern sky as they approached gate six at Belmont Park. The guard waved them through when Adam flashed his identification. The huge elm trees were still the same. Early morning track sounds hadn't changed. Horses whinnied. Someone was whistling as he walked a horse across the road. Someone else laughed. Only Trish's world had changed. She clamped down on the thought. No, her father wouldn't be back. The old litany started again. *Just get through!*

She greeted Patrick and sidestepped the hug he offered. Hugs were off limits. Spitfire was nearly her undoing. His familiar nicker and bobbing black head revealed his joy at seeing her. Trish wrapped both arms around the horse's neck and buried her face in his mane. One tear forced its way through her clenched eyelids. She hung on for dear life.

Spitfire raised his head and nibbled on her braid. When that didn't get her attention, he blew in her ear. Trish reached up to scratch behind his ears and down his cheek. His silent whuffle thanked her.

"How you been?" Trish whispered in his ear. Spitfire nodded and nosed her pocket for his carrot. "You miss me?" The black colt nodded again and rubbed his forehead against her chest. "Hasn't Patrick been treating you right?" Spitfire snorted.

"Sounds to me like you two carry on a pretty good conversation."

Trish spun around at the sound of the familiar voice. "Red!" She flung herself into his arms before she had time to think. Red held her close and pressed a kiss on her hair.

"How you doin'?" His whisper brushed the wisps of hair around her ear.

Trish just shook her head. She knew she had to get away from him before the tears started, but for a moment longer she clung in his embrace. Reluctantly, she pushed back and ducked under Spitfire's neck. If she bit her lip hard enough the tears retreated. Forced back by sheer force of will, again. She was getting better at this.

"You want to take Sarah's Pride while I ride Spitfire?

I'm sure she's ready for a run." She reached for the bridle Patrick handed to her. "How's she been doing?"

She could feel Red's stare boring holes into her back. How could she tell him that hugs and kind words were too much, even from him?

CHAPTER 5

Trish felt as if she were caught in a time warp.

Red whistled a popular tune as he rode beside her out to the track. Both the horses picked up the pace as they neared the mile-and-a-half oval. Cicadas chirped their way into the morning chorus as the sun hit the elm trees. The fragrance of the air was a combination of horse, freshly mown grass, and summer.

Nothing had changed. If Trish closed her eyes and pretended . . . She shook her head. No pretending, even if it did feel good.

She studied the space between Spitfire's ears. Everything had changed. She and Spitfire had run their last race. She bit down hard on her lip.

"What is it?" Red asked.

"Ummm, I was just thinking of the Breeder's Cup in October. Do you think we could run in it?"

"We?"

"Spitfire and me."

Red shook his head. "I wouldn't count on it. He's too valuable for stud now. The syndicate would never agree."

"I always thought he would be my horse. I mean, I knew he was good, and winning the Kentucky Derby and then the Triple Crown was a dream come true, but I never thought—" She squeezed her knees and Spitfire broke into a slow gallop.

"Thought what?" Sarah's Pride kept pace, snorting and fighting the bit to go faster. She surged ahead until Red pulled her back down.

Trish focused on the horses in front of them.

"Thought what, Trish? What were you thinking?"

"I never thought I would have to give him up . . . Have to live halfway across the country from him." She raised her voice to be heard above a horse grunting a hard gallop past them.

"You could always come and race in Kentucky."

"I thought about that." She pulled Spitfire back down to a walk. "But I have to finish high school first. My mom would never let me go now."

"Knock it off, horse." Red tightened his reins to keep the filly from chasing after another fast-working animal.

"You think she's ever gonna learn some manners?" Trish grabbed on to another topic. Racing and her mother were too close to home.

"Yeah, well, I tried. Now you get her. I'll watch for her name in the newspapers." Together they walked out the gate and down the narrow paved road to barn twelve.

With Patrick and Adam helping, they quickly had both horses washed, walked, and ready to load. The van arrived promptly at 7:00, just as they were all returning from the track kitchen and breakfast. Both horses walked up into the van without even a snort of temper or fear, much to Trish's surprise. Maybe Sarah's Pride was learning something after all.

"Trish, you and Red ride in the van, and Patrick and I'll drive the car, okay?" Adam looked up in time to catch the grin on Red's face. "Any problem with that?"

Red shook his head. "Nope." He grabbed Trish's hand and raised it with his. "Those horses may need these hands. We gotta be prepared."

When Red didn't let go of her hand, Trish tried to pull it away without being too obvious, but Red turned toward the van with her in tow. "Y'all drive safely now, ya hear?" Red waved with his free hand before opening the cab door for Trish.

The cicadas turned up the volume of their goodbye chorus as the van pulled out onto the street and headed for the Cross Island Expressway. They were on their way south, to Spitfire's new home.

Trish pulled out her internal telescope and flipped to the large end. Maybe that way she could ignore the friendly conversation between Red and Stokes, the van driver. And maybe if she concentrated hard enough she could sleep most of the trip. Maybe the moon was made of green cheese too.

Red was not easy to ignore.

Trish leaned her head back against the seat and instructed her muscles to relax. She concentrated on her hands, arms, legs, feet, willing each to relax.

Red told a joke and both men laughed. Trish felt herself smile. Red did tell a good story.

Back to relaxing. Trish felt warm and a bit floaty. Red's next story depended on his southern drawl for the punch line. He drew it out perfectly. A giggle started somewhere down about Trish's heels and bubbled its way up. She bit it back, but when Stokes came up with a topper she couldn't help it. The giggle escaped.

Red took her hand in his and stroked her fingers. She felt his smile and encouragement clear back down where that giggle had started. When she leaned back again, his arm cushioned her head.

His next joke was even more outrageous.

"You two trying to develop a comedy act or something?" she finally asked. "I think you could go on stage right now."

"Really?" Red drawled, wriggling his eyebrows like Groucho Marx.

Trish shook her head. "You're crazy, you know that?"

"Crazy about yoo-hoo-hoo-hoo," Red crooned. His eyebrows contorted again, and he let out a long yodel.

"I can't believe this." She stared from one to the other. "Did you two know each other before?"

"Before what?" Stokes raised his shoulders in a question.

"Before this trip!"

Red leaned forward to peer around Trish. "Do I know you, sir?"

"Beats me. Where'd you find her?"

"Hey, you're a poet!" They high-fived hands, nearly crushing Trish between them.

Trish groaned. "Hadn't you better think about driving?"

Stokes grinned at her, showing a chipped front tooth. Sandy hair curled from under his weathered and bent straw hat. "You doubtin' my driving?"

"No, it's just that—well—we had an accident on the way up this stretch of road and my dad . . ." The light went out again, and Trish bit down on her lip.

Nagger slipped in around her guard. *Here you are having a good time—laughing even—when you should be grieving for your father.* When she shuddered, Red's arm held her tighter. She couldn't look up to see the sympathy in his eyes. She just closed hers and prayed the miles would disappear. Maybe they should have flown the horses. But Spitfire hated loud noises, so her father had decided to truck him down.

Back to her father again. Everything always came back to him. Trish left off gnawing on her lip and attacked a torn cuticle on her left thumb.

When they stopped for lunch, they checked on the horses first. Spitfire nickered his welcome as soon as he heard Trish's voice. Sarah's Pride stamped her front foot and pawed at the rubber-coated flooring.

"You two behave now," Trish whispered as she gave Spitfire an extra scratching. He nudged her pocket, looking for the carrot she always carried. "Sorry, fella, I'm fresh out." She patted his rump on her way past. "You'll live without a treat this time." *That's something else to remember to tell the new groom. Always carry carrots.* Somehow the reminder didn't make her feel any better.

After pushing her lunch around on the plate so it looked like she'd eaten, Trish dug out her book bag before climbing back into the truck. But knowing she had to review for her finals, and doing it were two different things. Her eyes kept drooping shut. An hour or so down the road and the book clunked to the floor.

Red drew her over to rest on his shoulder as he leaned back against the door.

Darkness had fallen long before the truck turned onto New Circle Road, the highway that encircled Lexington. Stokes followed the signs to Old Frankfort Pike, right in the heart of bluegrass country. Headlights flashed on both black and white board fences as the road narrowed.

The BlueMist Farms sign leaped into the headlight glare. White board fences lined both sides of the long curving drive. A magnificent white house in traditional southern plantation style graced a knoll off to their right.

The road to the barns crossed a creek and passed a pond before ending in a graveled parking area.

Trish rubbed her eyes and stretched. While she'd only slept for a couple of hours, she felt as if they'd been in the truck for days. "What time is it?"

Red looked at his watch. "About ten-thirty. We made good time."

"Let's get them out and walk 'em around." Patrick stepped out of his car and arched his back. He and Stokes opened the doors to the van and slid out the ramp. The clanging of the metal sounded extra loud on the soft night air.

A pickup pulled into the paddock, its headlights trapping them in the intensity. As soon as the truck stopped, Donald Shipson stepped out and came forward to greet them. A short, wiry man, obviously an ex-jockey, joined him.

Trish tried to escape by ducking into the van, but Adam Finley took her arm and drew her back into the circle. She watched as Patrick and the new man slapped each other on the back.

"Can ya beat that?" Patrick beamed, his teeth gleaming in the car light. "Me old buddy, Timmy O'Ryan. Trish, meet the best man in the world to take care of Spitfire for you. Why, if I'da known . . ." He shook his head and slapped the man's back again.

Trish tried to swallow around the rock in her throat. Even she knew the name Timmy O'Ryan. While other kids collected baseball cards, Trish memorized racing times and the jockeys that set them. "I'm glad to meet you." Her voice came out strangled. "Ummm, excuse me, I need to see to Spitfire."

"Can I help you, Miss?" Timmy O'Ryan spoke with

the same soft lilt as Patrick. And he had the same steady, blue-eyed gaze. "Maybe he'll take to me better if you introduce us."

Trish nodded. Now she knew what a mouse caught in a trap must feel like.

Spitfire nickered his special welcome when Trish entered the van. He tossed his head, impatient to be free.

Timmy followed Trish as she patted her way up the horse's side to his head. "Hey, old fella, I have someone new for you to meet." She stroked the black's cheek and rubbed his ear.

Spitfire reached to sniff the hand the new man held out. He smelled the shirtsleeve and up to the porkpie hat, then down the other arm. Timmy stood perfectly still, but his voice seemed to whisper a love song as he and Spitfire became acquainted. At last he palmed a carrot and held it for the colt to munch.

"You've made a friend for life." Trish felt as if her forced smile would crack and her with it.

"Your father included suggestions like this in his letter of instructions. He wanted to make the transition as easy as possible."

Trish nodded. She turned to jerk the lead knot loose. "Come on, fella, back up."

Spitfire stopped in the doorway and trumpeted his arrival to any other horses who might be in the area. "Come on." Trish tugged on the lead. "You can quit showing off anytime."

Two answering whinnies came from the barn just past the gate. Spitfire raised his muzzle and sniffed the slight breeze to acquaint himself with the area. Then he followed Trish through the gate and around a second grassy paddock. Timmy loosely held the other lead and paced along with them.

"That's the stallion barn right over there." He pointed to a huge barn, shadowed now by the night. "He'll have his own paddock, and better care than most people give their kids. While I'm in charge of him, there'll be grooms helping me."

"He only lets me ride him."

"I understand. No one will ride him. We'll hand walk him or gallop him around the training track on a lead. You'll see, he'll get fat and sassy, but next spring when he goes to work, that'll change. I'll take care of him, Miss. You needn't worry."

Trish felt like the horses must feel as Timmy's gentle voice soothed her fears. Spitfire even drooped on the lead between them. "Come on, fella, let's see what your new home looks like."

She knew her eyes were big as tennis balls as she stared around the softly lit interior of the stallion barn. *People don't live this good*, she thought as she took in the glistening woodwork, the shiny brass fittings, and the gleaming name plates on spacious stalls. "There's yours." She pointed Spitfire's head toward the large box stall with *Spitfire* lettered in brass on an oval blue sign. "I can't believe this."

Timmy stopped beside her. "You think he'll be comfortable here?" Trish could hear the teasing in his voice before she saw the light dancing in his eyes.

"Most people wouldn't believe horses could live like this."

Timmy nodded. "His stall opens onto his own private two-acre paddock. There're shade trees down on the lower corner, and deep grass."

Trish looked up to see a huge picture of a blood bay, about a quarter of life-size.

"That's Shenandoah, the first stud here, and grandaddy to three Derby winners and countless others who did their share of winning on tracks all around the country." O'Ryan walked forward and swung open the door to Spitfire's stall. "Come on, let's see how he likes it."

Spitfire inspected every corner of his new home before returning to Trish for an ear-scratching. He draped his head over her shoulder, as if moving into a new stall was boring.

Trish felt the now familiar boulder clog her throat. She wouldn't feel his head on her shoulder anymore, not after tomorrow morning. She blinked hard and rolled her eyes toward the ceiling. *No! You can't cry now!* She sniffed once and felt herself gaining some measure of control.

"See you in the morning," she whispered in her horse's twitching ear. "You be good now." She gave him a last pat and closed the lower part of the stall door behind her. Spitfire hung his head over the door and whuffled his soundless nicker. Trish brushed past Timmy O'Ryan and headed for the exit. She was nearly running by the time she caught up with Red, who was still walking Sarah's Pride.

"Whoa, you okay?" Red stopped Trish with a hand on her arm. The filly threw her head up and danced sideways at the interruption. "Easy now." His soft voice worked for both the filly and Trish.

"H-have they said where we'll keep her?" Trish stammered before she got her voice under control.

"Yeah, there're stalls over there." Red pointed to a low building on the other side of the graveled area. "John and Adam went into the stallion barn just as you came out. Come on, let's put this girl away."

Sarah's Pride inspected her new quarters just as Spitfire had. She drank out of the tub in the corner and nibbled at the hay in the mesh sling. Trish and Red leaned on the closed stall door, watching her.

"Spitfire's going to be fine here, you know," Red broke the silence.

"I know."

"You can come and see him—and me."

"I will." Trish took a deep breath and turned around to lean against the wall. She studied the faint outline of the cupola-crested stallion barn. "Sure different than home." Her voice faded away on the slight breeze. She heard a frog chirp in the distance; a bullfrog answered. Sarah's Pride dribbled water on Trish's shoulder and in her hair. "Thanks a heap." Trish brushed it off and gave the filly a cheek scratch.

She pushed herself away from the wall, and she and Red walked out to join the men clustered around the pickup.

"Tim, you show Patrick and Red where they'll be sleeping, and, Stokes is it?" The driver nodded. "And Adam and Trish'll come with me." Donald Shipson waved toward the house Trish had seen when they drove up. "Breakfast will be served on the veranda from six to nine. Just come and help yourself."

"See you in the morning," Red whispered for Trish's ears alone as he squeezed her hand.

Trish nodded, then followed John and Adam to the car. Too tired to even appreciate the grand staircase to the upper floor, or the bedroom filled with antique furniture, it was all Trish could do to say good-night to Mrs. Shipson without yawning. She fell down that long black tunnel she'd come to appreciate.

A rooster crowing woke her in the morning. She slipped from the lace-draped four-poster bed and went to stand in front of the open window. Sheer white curtains drifted over her bare feet in the slight breeze. The sun arced high enough to jewel the dew on the manicured lawns and paddocks. Newly mown grass perfumed the air. Someone whistled a friendly tune off to the side of the grand house, and downstairs a bass voice sang the words. She could see the roof of the stallion barn through the trees.

Trish turned from all the peace and beauty to dress. Today she had to leave Spitfire.

"I'll drive you over to the barn if you'd like," the silver-haired Mr. Shipson said after greeting her at the bottom of the stairs.

"I was hoping to ride him, ahhh—" Trish swallowed her lump. "Uhhh . . . before we leave, if that's okay?"

"Of course. Timmy will ride with you and show you the way to the track. I think you'll be pleased when you see everything in daylight."

"You have an awesome place here." They stopped between the two center pillars on the front porch. Trish looked up at her host. "I've only seen spreads like this in pictures."

"Thank you. My family's owned this land since before The War."

"The war?"

"The Civil War." His smile twinkled in his eyes. "We forget the rest of the world doesn't count time from the War Between the States. My great-great-grandaddy founded the stud here." He stepped down to the first stair. "I can't imagine living anywhere else."

Trish followed her host out to the pickup, surprised

at how easy she felt with him. It was as if they'd known each other for a long time. She shook her head. And here she'd been all ready to dislike him—intensely. But she'd reminded herself that it wasn't his fault Spitfire was coming here and not back to Vancouver.

It was my father's fault, actually. He had started the syndication. Trish suddenly felt betrayed. Why had he done this to her? Her vision blurred so she could hardly see the sweeping drive, the stream, and the glass-like pond. She sank back into the seat.

"Trish? Are you all right?"

"Uh, yeah." She shook her head, trying to clear away the fog.

"I know leaving Spitfire here must be terrible for you. I wish there was some way I could help—"

You could let him go home with me. The words were so clear in her head Trish was afraid she'd shouted them.

"I want you to understand that you are welcome to visit here any time you'd like. If you want to come to Kentucky to race, I'll do whatever I can to help you. Spitfire is still your horse, you know."

Only part of him. Again Trish bit down on her tongue so as not to verbalize the words.

"Our home is yours. Both my wife and I would love having you here." Donald braked the truck and turned off the ignition. "I mean it Trish; this isn't just southern hospitality talking."

"Thank you." Trish took a deep breath. "I'll remember that." She could feel her smile tremble at the edges. "Thanks."

Timmy and Patrick had Sarah's Pride and another horse saddled, and Patrick slipped a bridle over Spitfire's ears just as he whinnied his welcome to Trish.

"Right in my ear," Patrick grumbled. The next instant his hat went bowling across the floor. "Had to get one in, didn't you?"

Trish stooped down to pick up Patrick's stained and wrinkled fedora. "I keep telling you to watch it." She handed the hat back to Patrick, her grin securely in place. Spitfire's clowning made everything easier. "Had to get him, didn't you?" She rubbed under Spitfire's forelock and got a grainy lick for her efforts.

Red walked up with three helmets. He handed one to Trish and one to Timmy, then put on his own. "Hi, how d'ya like the summer morning? No other place like this on earth."

"You're prejudiced. You haven't seen a sunny morning in Washington yet." Trish walked between the two men, Spitfire tagging behind her.

Patrick gave her a leg up. "Now don't be takin' too long," he said softly. "We need to be loading the girl here and heading for the airport."

"I know." The sun seemed to dim.

"This way," Timmy said from the back of his bay as he led the way through an open gate and between two white board fences. He pointed out the other four stallions and a field of mares and foals. While Red asked questions, Trish grew more quiet, savoring each moment. She listened with one ear, and planted each tree and fencepost in her memory so she could visualize Spitfire being worked on this track. Spitfire's stall, his paddock, his barn, the smell of the grass, the song of the birds.

How could she leave him here? It was too much to ask.

CHAPTER 6

What was left of Trish's heart felt twisted and torn.

"Y'all come back now," Mrs. Shipson said, giving Trish a warm hug. "As Donald said, our home is yours—any time." She stepped back and shook hands with Patrick, and Adam Finley. "Y'all take care now."

Trish waved as she stepped up into the truck. Her blurry vision made her stub her toe on the step.

Red caught her and helped her into the cab. "You okay?"

Trish just nodded. She fought the tears, teeth clamped so hard her jaw ached. As they drove down the fence-lined drive she stared at the clock on the dashboard. Hands tucked under her arms, she shivered once. Red laid his arm across the back of the seat and massaged her neck.

All Trish could see on the back of her eyelids was Spitfire galloping across his new paddock. She could hear his whinny; feel his last whiskery whuffle. A lone tear squeezed past her iron control gate and meandered down her cheek.

Red brushed it away with one gentle finger.

———

"I meant it, Trish, about coming to California and

racing for me this summer," Adam Finley said just before he boarded his plane in Lexington. "I know it's going to be rough for you in the days ahead, and new scenery might make your summer easier."

"I—I have to finish my finals, and then I promised my mom I'd take chemistry at Clark College. She'll never let me out of that."

"Well, just remember we have colleges in California, too. I'm sure you could find a class in the evening." He reached as if to hug her then drew back. "I know how hard you are fighting this, Trish. Martha and I would love to be able to help you, and you would be helping us too. Your dad's passing has left a mighty big hole—in many lives."

"Ahhh . . ." Trish nodded instead of trying to finish her thought. "Thanks for all you've done for us." She looked up to see tears glistening in Adam's eyes.

"Crying isn't a sin, my dear." Finley sniffed and blinked a couple of times. "No matter how hard you fight it, letting the tears come will help you get better."

Trish shook her head. Her strangled "I can't" carried from over her shoulder as she headed for the exit.

She had her armor back in place by the time she joined Red and Patrick at the cargo dock.

Loading Sarah's Pride on the plane proved surprisingly easy. Patrick had come prepared with a tranquilizer shot, but the filly walked up the ramp with only a snort and a toss of her head. Once inside, she trembled and broke into a sweat while the men erected the stall around her, but she stood still. With Red doing the same on the other side of the horse, Trish rubbed the filly's neck and ears. At the same time she whispered her soothing monologue, the song she'd learned from her father.

"I'll call you soon." Red ducked under the horse's neck after she'd lipped a bit of hay from the sling. He put one arm around Trish and brushed a strand of hair off her cheek with his other hand.

"Okay." One word was all Trish could manage.

"You'll write or call? You can always get in touch with me through my mom and dad."

Trish nodded. Red raised her chin and brushed her lips with his. She turned her head before he could kiss her again and shatter her control. Leaving hurt so bad. How much more could she stand?

Red squeezed her shoulder. "Take care." He levered himself over the stall.

Trish heard him say goodbye to Patrick. If she started to cry now, she knew she'd never be able to stop. *Just get through*. The inner order worked again.

The filly swung her rear end from side to side as the plane revved for takeoff. Patrick joined Trish in the box to try to keep the horse calm. Together they kept her from slipping as the plane floor slanted. When the plane leveled off, the horse quieted down. She sighed and dropped her head, as if all the tension had worn her out.

Trish stretched and wrapped both arms around her shoulders to pull the kinks out. She dropped her chin on her chest, then shrugged her shoulders to her ears.

"Ye did a good job, lass." Patrick walked around the filly, adjusting the travel sheet as he checked for any more sweating. He unbuckled the crimson blanket and pulled it off. "She needs a dry one after all that."

Trish handed him the extra sheet and helped buckle it.

"It'll get easier, lass, take my word for it."

Trish just shook her head.

"You want to go sit down for a while? I'll stay with the girl here."

"No. You do that." Trish dug a brush out of the tack bucket. "It helps me to keep busy." She flipped back the sheet over one front quarter and started brushing.

The remainder of the trip passed without incident. Trish spent part of the time studying, but failed to turn many pages. Her eyelids kept drooping.

David had the six-horse trailer ready and waiting when they landed at Portland International Airport. Unloading and reloading went without a hitch, and they were crossing the I–205 bridge within a few minutes. The overcast skies seemed to match Trish's overcast disposition.

She let Patrick tell about their trip to Kentucky and describe BlueMist Farms. She was back at the other end of the telescope, looking and listening from a great distance. It was easier that way.

David pointed out the sights to Patrick. Trish could feel her brother studying her between comments, but she shut her eyes and ignored him.

It wasn't so easy to ignore her mother. Marge met them when they drove down to the barns at Runnin' On Farm. She hugged her daughter once, then a second time before Trish could slip past.

Trish caught herself looking around for her father. Quickly she knelt to hug her dog, Caesar, and ruffle his pristine white ruff. The collie responded by quick-licking her cheek.

"I know, Tee." Marge stood beside Trish with her hands in the back pockets of her jeans. "I keep looking for him, too."

A knife-sharp pain stabbed Trish. She felt as if her

heart couldn't take any more blows. She knew if she said anything or looked at the pain in her mother's eyes, she'd crumble and lose the control she'd worked so hard to maintain.

Instead, she bit down on her lip and ducked her head as she followed David into the van to bring out Sarah's Pride. *Spitfire should be coming home, too.* Where was the celebration? Who could celebrate? She stomped her rampaging feelings down into a steel box somewhere in her middle and bolted the lid.

"Easy now." David smoothed the filly's neck as he jerked loose the tie rope. "Welcome to your new home."

Welcome to nothing. Trish caught the words before she spoke them aloud. She could hear her mother and Patrick talking outside the van. She untied the opposite lead and kept pace as David led their new arrival out the door.

Sarah's Pride minced down the ramp and danced around in a circle, head up, surveying the area. She whinnied and pawed one front foot.

"Her stall is all ready," David said. "I figured we should keep her separated from the others for a while."

"You're right, boy." Patrick patted the horse's right shoulder. "Why don't you lead her around for a bit and let her work off some of her energy. We'll give her a real work tomorrow and see if we can't finish breaking some of her bad habits." He tipped his fedora back on his head. "She sure is a determined one."

"Well, stubborn fits right into this family," Marge said. "She ran well the last time she was out, though, didn't she?"

Trish felt her jaw drop in amazement. Since when had her mother cared anything about how a horse ran?

She caught a grin that David tried to hide behind the filly's neck. What was going on here? Her brother trotted off with the horse in tow.

"Patrick, I think Hal told you that we'd ordered a mobile home for you." Marge leaned against the truck's front fender. "The people installing the septic tank will be here tomorrow. The power and phone will be in by the end of the week, and the trailer should be here Friday, too. In the meantime, you can have David's room. He'll take the couch."

"No, no." Patrick shook his head. "Ye needn't be putting yourself out like that. I'll just fix a cot down here and . . ."

"No, Patrick. This is the way Hal would want it. We had planned to have everything ready before you arrived, but . . ." she raised her hands in a helpless shrug, ". . . we'll make do until then. You're a member of our family, and while the kids used to have slumber parties down in the barn, you'll be much more comfortable up at the house."

Trish could hardly believe her ears. Who *was* this person who'd taken over her mother's body? And her mouth? Trish looked up in time to catch her mother wiping away a tear from the corner of her eye. Patrick looked misty-eyed too.

Trish dashed after David. "I'll see if he needs help." But David already had the filly loosed in her stall and was closing the lower half of the stall door.

"You know, I thought about bringing Dan'l up to keep her company, but Mom said to wait a couple of days. She's right, of course." David checked the latch and turned toward the house. "I've already done all the other chores."

"All right, what's going on here?" Trish kicked some gravel off to the side.

"What do you mean?"

"You know. Since when has Mom cared about what goes on down here?"

"Down here?" David picked up a stone and pegged it up the driveway.

"David!" Trish jerked on his arm.

"Okay, okay." He raised his hands in surrender. "We had a long talk, Mom and I, and she said it was time she learned more about the horses and racing—since she doesn't want to sell the farm. . . ."

Trish breathed a deep sigh of relief.

"You thought she might, didn't you?"

"It crossed my mind." Trish shoved her fingers into her pockets.

"Well, she isn't. She said she and Dad had talked it all over. He told her to sell if she wanted to."

Trish felt a boot-kick in her gut. *Her father had said that?*

"But Mom says she wants to keep the farm; that with Patrick's experience, and maybe hiring some more help when I leave for school . . ."

She felt the kick again. "But, I—you—but . . ." David couldn't leave too.

"I know." David stopped and picked up another piece of crushed rock. He ran his finger over the rough edges. "But Mom said . . ."

Trish felt an arrow of anger again, the sharp one that caused her to clench her teeth. Since when did her mother know all about what was best for everybody? That was her dad's job. She yanked her mind back to what David was saying.

" . . . we had to pick up our lives and go on. My goal has always been to be a veterinarian, and now I want to specialize in equine medicine. You knew that."

Trish nodded. She kicked another rock and watched it bounce off into the grass. *Sure, pick up their lives and go on. He made it sound so easy. As if the world hadn't totally fallen apart.*

"I know this is hard for you, Tee."

She shook her head. "Yeah." *You don't know the half of it, buddy-boy. What do you think you're doing, just making plans like—like . . .*

"Trish, Dad would want us to get on with our lives, too—school, racing, all of it."

Trish flung away his arm when he reached out to touch her. "Easy for you to say. You just go away and step back into a life that didn't include us anyway. And Mom—she just acts like everything is fine. Well it's not. It'll never be fine again!" She felt like planting her fist in the middle of her brother's nose.

Caesar whimpered at Trish's harsh voice. He nudged her fist with his cold nose and whined again. When she ignored him, he tried a sharp bark.

Trish dropped to her knees and buried her face in the collie's heavy ruff. When David laid a hand on Trish's head, she shook it away. "Just leave me alone. Everyone, just leave me alone."

And that's what she felt like when she walked into the house. Alone. Her dad wasn't sitting in his recliner. He'd never sit in his chair again.

CHAPTER 7

"Trish, I'm so glad you're here." Rhonda threw her arms around her friend.

"Yeah, me too." Trish stuffed her book bag into her locker. At least Prairie High hadn't changed in the month or so she'd been gone. Kids still bumped into each other in the halls, yelled across the commons, and rushed off to class when the bell rang. She kept expecting everything to be different, just because she was.

"Can I help you somehow?" Rhonda clutched her books to her chest.

Trish shook her head. She seemed to be doing a lot of that lately. "David says just to pick up our lives and go on. That's what Dad would want." She felt like slamming her locker door and running screaming down the hall. "So my dad died. So what's the big deal?" Trish lifted her chin in the air and glared at her friend.

"Tee, you know David didn't mean it like that," Rhonda scolded.

"We'd better get to class. I've got a final first period. I can't wait till this is over."

Others looked the other way when they caught Trish's eye. There would be no "welcome home" or congratulations this time.

Rhonda stopped Trish before she entered her first-period class. "They don't know what to say, Tee. None of us do."

"Yeah, congratulations doesn't fit, does it." Trish shifted her books to the other arm. "Forget it, Rhonda. Just ace your test."

Trish had a hard time focusing on the test paper in front of her. The words ran together. They carried no meaning. She glanced up at the clock. Fifteen minutes had passed; she'd written down one answer. Her jaw was beginning to ache from being clenched so tight, but Trish used the pain to help her focus. She *would not* fail these tests. She was tough—wasn't she?

Brad was waiting outside the school in his Mustang at the end of the day. Trish dropped like a stone onto the front seat.

"Pretty bad, huh?"

She exhaled and leaned her head back on the seat. "Worse."

"I'll bet they'd give you an extension if you asked." Brad tilted his seat forward so Rhonda could get in the back.

"Mrs. Olson told me she would. But I'd rather tough it out and get done."

"How's it feel to be done with high school?" Rhonda asked Brad, blowing upward to lift her bangs.

"Good. I just came back to gloat over you guys still struggling with finals. I also knew you wouldn't want to take the bus."

"Thanks," Trish said. "I don't think I could have handled the bus ride today. I was hoping to have my new convertible, but they aren't in yet."

"You think your mom will let you drive it to school?"

"I think she's going to have a cow every time I get in it."

"You want to study together? I can come over."
Rhonda leaned her chin on the back of the front seat.

"No—I don't think so. I'm so tired; I'm going to bed.
I'll probably study later." *If at all. Who cares, anyway?*
Trish's thoughts seemed louder than her voice.

That evening her mom woke her to say Red was on
the phone. Trish stumbled into the kitchen and sank
down on the floor to lean against the oak cabinets, the
phone clamped between her ear and her shoulder.

"How's my girl?" Red's voice sounded as if he were
in the next room.

"Sleepy." Trish couldn't control a yawn. "I had two
finals today; I have two tomorrow, and two on Wednesday. I'll be glad when they're over."

"I won today, and a place in the seventh. How about
that for some good news?"

"Bet the winner's circle felt good." Trish yawned
again. " 'Scuse me. I just can't wake up."

"I miss you."

Trish felt a little twinge of guilt. She hadn't even
thought about Red since she left him at the airport.
"Yeah, so how's it look for you. Lots of mounts?" She
forced herself to stay with the conversation but couldn't
think of anything to say. When the silence stretched for
several seconds, she mumbled, "Well, I'll talk to you
later; I need to hit the books." She hung up the phone as
if it were a fifty-pound weight.

Man, he's gonna think you don't even like him, Nagger
jumped right in. Trish had been able to shut him off
lately, but even that was too much trouble tonight.

She sat down at her desk to study but found herself
staring at the wall instead. Maybe if she propped herself
against the headboard of her bed . . .

Her mother found her there, sound asleep, with her history book on the floor. Trish hadn't even heard it drop.

"How about crawling under the covers?" Marge smoothed wisps of hair back from Trish's cheek.

"I need to study." Trish stretched and yawned. "I'm just so tired."

"I know. Maybe you should take incompletes and . . ."

"No. I just want to get school over with. I didn't do so bad today, at least I don't think so." She swung her feet to the floor. "Maybe if I tank up on Diet Coke I can stay awake."

————

Trish fell asleep the next day during study hall.

"You want to run the track with me instead of lunch?" Trish asked Rhonda when they met at their lockers for break.

"Let's grab a sandwich and then I will. I'm starved. We'll have to run fast." Rhonda stuffed her money in her pocket and her books in her locker.

A brisk breeze scattered clouds across the sky and blew their hair in their eyes as Trish and Rhonda ran the cinder track behind the brick complex. They jogged the first lap, stretched some, and ran the second.

Rhonda puffed to a halt and grabbed her side. "Owww. We need to do this more often or not at all."

Trish sucked in huge gulps of air. "Want to go another?"

"You crazy?" Rhonda folded in half and wrapped her arms around her knees to stretch again. "If that didn't wake you up, nothing will. Besides," she glanced at her watch, "we have ten minutes till the bell, and I'm spending mine eating."

Trish shivered as the breeze blew through her wet shirt.

"Here." Rhonda handed her a jacket. "We can walk and chew at the same time, or at least we used to be able to." She grabbed Trish who tripped on a sprinkler head. "Ya gotta pay attention."

Those words haunted Trish all afternoon. Why couldn't she pay attention? Why did her mind seem to wander off all on its own? And she wasn't even thinking of anything, just wandering in a black fog. She felt better at the end of the day, however. She knew she'd aced the history test. All those hours of studying while she'd been traveling had paid off.

That evening she ran down the drive, up to Brad's, and back to their own barn to see Miss Tee. The filly snorted and dashed off to circle the pasture before coming to nibble her treat from Trish's hand.

"You sure are a beauty." Trish rubbed the filly's velvety cheek and inhaled the wonderful odor of horse.

"She has good speed for a baby," Patrick leaned on the fence beside her. "Good motion too. You can tell she loves to run; already makes sure she finishes first against Double D. 'Course he's a tad younger."

"She should be good. Her dam has thrown two colts. One Dad sold as a yearling—he's running at Long Acres, won a couple; and the other went back to Minnesota, I think. Last I heard he was doing okay, too. Dad said all our money went into stud fees the last couple of years. He knew it was necessary if we wanted to go someplace besides Portland Meadows."

"Well, looks to be paying off." Patrick tipped his hat back and scratched his head. "We got a lot of work to do, soon as you're done with school."

That night Trish turned her light off just after midnight. It looked like running was the answer—to staying awake, that is.

———————

By Wednesday evening she felt brain-dead and ready to skip the last half-day of school. But her finals and her junior year were finished.

"How does it feel to be a big senior?" Rhonda asked as she dug the last candy wrapper out of the back of her locker.

"I don't feel any different . . ." Trish scraped at a piece of tape that had held the school calendar on the inside of her locker door. ". . . other than being totally beat."

"You want to go to a movie tonight? The four musketeers haven't done anything together for a long time." Rhonda slammed her locker shut and wiped her hands on the back of her jeans.

Trish shook her head.

"The mall?"

"I don't think so. Let's get outta here."

———————

The sun hadn't broken through the overcast the next morning before Trish was galloping through the ground fog on Sarah's Pride. Patrick had decreed long gallops to build stamina for all three horses. Owner, John Anderson, decided to return Gatesby to Runnin' On Farm now that Patrick was the trainer, so Trish had the gelding and Firefly to work too. She could hear Patrick muttering as she walked the filly back to the barns.

David was trying hard to keep a straight face.

"Gatesby at it again?" she asked as she leaped to the ground.

"No manners. All we need is a cockeyed plug with a sense of humor. If I didn't know . . ." Patrick glared at Trish and then David. "And don't say I told you so, either." He picked up his hat and beat it against his leg. "Fat and sassy, that's all he is. Well, son," he said staring into the gelding's right eye, "you hear me now and listen up good. I won't tolerate that kind of nonsense."

Gatesby pulled his head as high as the tie rope permitted, and rolled his eyes till the whites showed.

Trish chuckled at the familiar sight. She looked around to share the joke with her father, and the moment popped like a shimmery soap bubble on a breeze. She lifted her knee for David to boost her up. The rock lodged back in her throat.

When she returned from the gallop, David and Patrick were discussing Long Acres versus going to California to race with Adam Finley.

"Which would you rather do, lass?" Patrick asked as he tossed Trish aboard Firefly.

"Whatever."

"You must have an opinion."

Trish shook her head. "I don't really care."

That seemed to be her theme song. At least she heard herself saying it more than once a day. And she thought it a lot more often. Why should she care? Why bother?

On Friday the dealer called to say he had three red convertibles sitting on his lot waiting for them.

"What time would you like to pick them up?" the man asked.

74

"Two be okay?" Trish said, after checking with David and her mother.

"You want to invite Brad and Rhonda to go along?" Marge asked when Trish hung up the phone.

"Is Patrick coming?" Trish drew circles in a puddle of water on the counter.

"That's up to you."

"Whatever . . ."

"No. *You* have to make a decision. We can turn this into a celebration like it should be or you can play 'whatever.' " Marge crossed her arms and leaned back against the kitchen counter. "It's up to you."

How can we celebrate when he's not here? Trish thought as she glared at her mother. She slapped her hand in the water, spraying it over the counter. "Fine. We'll invite everybody. Make it a big party. Winner of the Triple Crown—and it doesn't mean squat. Nothing means anything anymore, don't you know that?" Her voice rose to a shriek as she charged through the living room and down the hall to her bedroom. She slammed the door and threw herself across the bed, only to pound her fists on the floor.

"Sorry," she muttered an hour or so later when she came back to the kitchen.

"I know you are. It helps to get the anger out." Marge shut the oven after removing a sheet of chocolate chip cookies. Her eyes were red-rimmed like she'd been crying. She set the cookie tray on the counter and reached for a tissue to blow her nose.

"It's easier if we help each other. So far you haven't let any of us close enough to help you." She dabbed at the corners of her eyes.

"I can't," Trish choked out. "I'd better call Rhonda and Brad. Where's Patrick?"

"Down watching them set up his new home. He's hoping to sleep there tonight."

Later, in the station wagon on the way into Vancouver, Rhonda asked, "What are you gonna do with the third car, give it to the church?"

Trish stared at Rhonda like she'd dropped her remaining marbles. "I wouldn't give God the time of day if He asked, let alone a car!"

"Trish!"

"Well, would you?" Trish slumped lower in her seat and chewed on her thumbnail.

"I thought maybe our youth group could get a used van with the money from the sale of the car. You'd said you might give it to the church."

"Yeah, well, God can buy a van for the church."

"Attitude . . ." Brad poked Trish in the ribs from the other side. "Your dad wouldn't be very happy to hear that."

Trish folded her arms across her chest and glared up at her friend. What right did he, or anyone for that matter, have to tell her what her father would want?

Nagger got her attention. *You know your dad always gave of himself and what he had to help others.*

When they walked into the showroom, they were met by reporters and a television camera. Trish was surprised, and plastered a smile on her face.

"Yes, the second one goes to my brother David here. He earned it. . . . No, I don't know what to do with the third one. Guess I'll decide later."

"Where are you racing next?" a man asked around his camcorder.

Trish shook her head. "I—we're not sure yet."

"How'd you feel about leaving Spitfire in Kentucky?"

"I—I . . ." She shot a pleading look at Patrick and David.

David stepped forward. "Of course it was hard for Trish to leave her horse in Kentucky, but we know that's what's best for Spitfire."

"You still thinking of the Breeder's Cup?"

"No, that's out now." David took Trish by the arm. "How about letting us get our cars?"

Laughter rippled across the balloon-decked room. The camera held on Trish and David as they accepted the keys from the dealer, and followed them outside to the cars. Sunlight bounced off the windshield and sparkled on the cherry-red finish.

A reporter opened the door for Trish and winked at her as she slid onto the smooth black leather seat. "How's it feel?" he asked.

Trish placed both hands on the steering wheel. She adjusted the seat and turned the ignition key. "Fantastic." She smiled into the camera. "Come on, Rhonda. You get to ride first."

Rhonda slid in next to her. "Awesome." She stroked the gleaming dashboard. "Wow."

Trish waved at David and Brad in the next car. "See you guys."

"Drive carefully," Marge couldn't resist saying as they drove out onto the street.

Trish tooted the horn. "Shall we see how fast it'll go?"

"I wouldn't," Rhonda giggled. "Every cop in Clark County's gonna be watching for that hot young jockey with the red convertible."

"Where shall we go?"

"I don't know but don't look back, we're being followed."

"Meet you at the Burgerville in Orchards," Brad called as he and David pulled up alongside them.

"Yeah, we'll let *him* get the ticket." Trish hit the horn again, then stopped just as the light ahead turned red. A car full of boys behind them honked and waved. When Rhonda turned to look, they whistled and honked again.

"You know, this could get kinda fun." Rhonda settled back in her seat, grinning from ear to ear.

"What do you mean by that?"

"Well, I mean . . . we might meet some new guys. . . . Who knows?"

If only my dad were here, Trish swallowed the thought. *He'd be teasing Rhonda and me right now.* She drove into the restaurant parking lot. More guys were clustered around Brad and David's car.

"See?" Rhonda nodded at the scene. "Red convertibles *attract* guys."

Trish spotted a familiar station wagon on the other side of the parking lot and pulled in next to it. She didn't want the extra attention.

But she couldn't turn off the congratulations of the Prairie High students who were gathered inside. She glued her smile in place until she could hide behind a hot fudge sundae.

"What are you gonna name it?" Rhonda licked her spoon and stared at Trish's puzzled look. "The car, silly. You have to give it a name."

They hadn't come up with a good one by the time Trish dropped Rhonda off at home.

That evening Marge called a family meeting. "I think we need to lay some ground rules about the cars," she said as they gathered around the dining room table.

Trish tried to ignore the empty place where her father

always sat. Patrick occupied the chair beside her. She listened with only half an ear, because she already knew what the rules would be. No picking up riders, no speeding, no crazy driving—as if Trish would do any of those things. She nodded in all the right places.

"Now, about the summer . . ." Marge folded her hands on the table in front of her. "What do you think of taking the summer off and not racing anywhere until Portland Meadows opens in the fall?"

Trish shrugged.

"Maybe my opinion's out of place," Patrick said carefully, "but it'd be a shame not to race those three. They'll be ready in a couple of weeks."

"Dad had planned on Long Acres," David put in. "We could go up just for the races we enter."

"There's always California," Patrick spoke again, not sure of his place in the decision. "You know Adam wants Trish to come down there."

"Trish promised to take a class at Clark College this summer to make up chemistry," Marge spoke in her my-mind's-made-up tone.

Trish felt like an invisible child. Everyone seemed to be talking around her, as if they all knew what was best for her.

"Well, we could just ship the three horses to California, and let Adam take care of them." David rubbed the bridge of his nose. "That would make it easier for everyone."

Trish jerked alive. "*I* ride our horses." She stood up so fast her chair fell backward. "Where the horses go, I go." She stalked out of the room.

CHAPTER 8

Trish felt like kicking her bedroom door shut.

Her eyes burned. Her throat felt tight as if she were being strangled. When there was a knock at her door she muttered, "Leave me alone."

"Trish . . ." Marge tapped again, then opened the door.

"I said, leave me alone." Trish stared out the window, her knuckles white as they gripped the sill.

"I've tried that; it isn't working." Marge sat down on Trish's bed.

Silence hung in the room, like the oppression before a summer storm.

"Tee, I . . ."

"Don't call me that!" Trish whirled around. "That was Dad's name for me. And he's not here!"

"I know, Trish, but . . ."

"I can't stand it! You all talk as if nothing's happened. *Trish is taking chemistry. We could ship the horses to California.*" Her voice rose as she spoke. "I can't take any more of this."

"It's not easy for any of us, Trish. You aren't the only one affected." Marge straightened up on the bed, trying to control her own emotions. "We're all doing the best we can with a situation none of us likes. Do you think your father *wanted* to die and leave us all?"

"Well, he did, didn't he?" Trish turned back to the window, unable to face the tears streaming down her mother's face. The desire to fling herself into her mother's arms was strong, but she hung on to the windowsill, unable to let down the floodgate of her own tears.

Finally Marge sighed and pulled a tissue from the nightstand. "Trish, I understand your anger, but you can't keep taking it out on the rest of us. We're trying to get through ourselves, and we want to help you."

"Don't."

Marge stood and joined her daughter at the window. "How about talking with Pastor Mort?"

Trish shook her head. "No way."

When Marge tried to give her a hug, Trish sidestepped so it turned into a pat on the shoulder.

"I need to go see how Miss Tee is."

The next morning, after long gallops on the three horses in training, plus a nip from Gatesby, Trish took a lead shank out to the pasture and waited for Miss Tee to meet her at the fence. The filly danced up and stopped just out of reach. She extended her muzzle in search of a treat, but leaped away when Trish reached for the halter.

"Great. This is turning into a perfect morning." Trish forced herself to stand perfectly still and wait for the filly to come to her; her patience lasting only long enough for Miss Tee to sniff her hand for the usual carrot.

"Sorry, you didn't earn one today." She snapped the lead shank in place and led the filly through the gate.

"Where you going?" David asked when Trish continued past the barns and toward the drive.

"Taking her for a long walk. She needs to learn some manners."

"Well, take her around the track then."

"David, quit the boss stuff. I know what I'm doing." She clucked to the filly and walked off. She could hear David muttering and complaining but chose to ignore both him and Patrick. "You're my horse, you'd think I could do what I want." Miss Tee bumped her head against Trish's shoulder as if begging for her treat. Trish gave her a small piece of carrot.

Her dog, Caesar, padded beside them as they alternately trotted and walked down the long gravel driveway. "Come on, Miss Tee," Trish encouraged the filly, "you have to do the same thing I do." She tugged on the lead shank to pick up the pace. Miss Tee pulled her head up and back, ears flat, each time the lead shank tightened over her nose. Trish patted her neck. "You're just making life miserable for yourself. *Go along with me; it's easier.*"

Trish turned forward and clucked with a tug again. They were nearly at the Runnin' On Farm sign; time to turn back. At the instant she turned, a rabbit dashed across the drive in front of them. Caesar exploded after the rabbit, his sharp bark cutting the air.

Miss Tee bolted. Her shoulder spun Trish around sending her to her knees. The force ripped the lead shank from her hands, and the filly tore out onto the road, swerving just in time to avoid broadsiding an oncoming car.

The filly whinnied in fear, the lead shank slapping her on the side, and galloped up the road.

Trish felt as if she were watching a horror movie in

slow motion. She leaped to her feet and dashed after the horse.

"Can we help you?" the driver of the car stopped to ask. "I thought we'd hit her for sure."

"If you could wait here . . . no, back there on the other side of our driveway and stop any oncoming cars . . ." Trish pointed behind her.

"Okay." The man backed up.

Trish ran on ahead. She could see Miss Tee just over the rise, still running hard. A horn honked. Brakes squealed.

Trish poured on all the speed she had, terrified she'd find the filly crushed on the road ahead.

She topped the rise. A car was swerved sideways in the road, but the filly ran on.

Each breath burned her lungs as Trish sucked in great gulps of air, still pounding up the road. Then she heard a vehicle pulling up beside her.

"Trish, for Pete's sake, get in!" David stopped the truck long enough for Trish to jump on the running board and hang on to the doorframe. "I told you . . ." David clipped off his words. "What happened?"

"A rabbit ran out and Caesar chased it. Miss Tee spooked. I'll never forgive myself if something happens to her."

Another car was stopped in the road ahead of them, the driver waving his arms to stop the rampaging horse. Miss Tee swerved to the side and galloped up the driveway to Brad's house.

"Thank you, thank you, thank you," Trish muttered, totally unaware that she was praying in spite of herself.

Brad had heard the commotion and swung open the gate to the corral by the barn. Miss Tee dodged away from his waving arms and into the corral.

Trish leaped to the ground as David slammed on the brakes.

"I'm going back to thank those people who helped us," David called as he backed out the driveway.

The filly stood spraddle-legged in the center of the dirt pen. Her head drooped, sides heaving as she struggled to catch her breath.

Trish and Brad slowly walked up to her on either side, both talking gently. Lather flecked both flanks and chest of the weary filly. Only her ears flicked back and forth to show she knew they were there. When Trish caught the lead shank under Miss Tee's chin, she trembled but stood still.

"I'll get another," Brad murmured when Trish had the horse secured. He returned in seconds with another shank to clip on.

All the while Trish crooned her song in the filly's twitching ears; scolding, but soothing. "You crazy horse, you've seen rabbits before. Boy, are we in for it now."

"What happened? How'd she get loose?" Brad stroked Miss Tee's sweaty neck.

"Don't ask." Trish shook her head. "Hang on tight, okay?" When Brad had the strap secure, she squatted down to run her hands over the filly's legs, checking for any strains.

David joined them in the corral. "She okay?" At Trish's nod, he let out a breath.

Trish looked up. A thundercloud was perched on David's forehead; she knew lightning was about to strike.

"If you two lead her, I'll drive in front to protect you. I don't think we need to bring the trailer over."

"That okay with you?" Trish asked Brad.

"Sure."

Miss Tee released a huge sigh and nuzzled Trish's pocket for a carrot. While she munched the treat, she rubbed her forehead against Trish's shoulder.

The trek home passed without incident. Brad didn't let go until the filly was safely housed in one of the stalls.

"For crying out loud, Trish!" David slammed his fist against the wall. "You know better than that. I told you not to take her out. Where's your head? You could have gotten her killed; yourself, too."

Patrick handed Trish a bucket of warm water. "Let's get her washed down and blanketed."

"She's not hurt," Trish snapped back. "And you don't have to tell me how stupid I was; I already know that."

Brad took the bucket from Trish, and he and Patrick each took a side of the filly and went to work.

"You don't know she's not hurt, and now she'll probably be scared to death of cars and everything else. She could be wind-broken for all we know."

"Quit yelling at me! You're not perfect, either."

"You deserve to be yelled at. You were totally irresponsible. Dad woulda had your hide."

"If you two are going to fight, move it away from here," Patrick interrupted. "You're scaring her again."

"Fine." Trish spun on her heel and jogged up the rise to the house.

"We're not finished yet!" David called after her.

"Oh, yes we are." She pounded up the stairs and burst through the door.

"What happened?" Marge turned, her face in a frown.

"Ask David. He has all the answers." In her room, Trish pulled her suitcase off the closet shelf. She threw in jeans, T-shirts, and underwear. She was pulling blouses off hangers when her mother entered the room.

"Where are you going?"

"Kentucky." Trish rolled a sweatshirt and stuffed it in a corner of the case.

"What do you mean by that?"

"I mean I'm going to see Spitfire. The Shipsons invited me to come anytime, and I'm going."

"Trish, this is crazy." Marge stood between her daughter and the suitcase. "You're not going anywhere. That college class starts next week, and you've work to do here besides."

"Mother, listen to me. I cannot stay here another minute. I'm going stark-raving mad. Today I did something so stupid it almost cost us a horse. Everywhere I look I expect to see Dad, and he's not here. Right now, I wouldn't even want to see him."

"Well, you're *not* going to Kentucky. We can work this out."

"No." Trish shook her head. "I can't stand to stay here. Let me go see if Spitfire is all right."

"You don't have a ticket. It'll cost a fortune." Marge sank down on Trish's bed.

"You've forgotten, I have money now. More money than any girl needs." Trish dusted off her riding boots and added them to the bag.

"No. I just can't see it, Trish." Marge covered her face with her hands. "Not now, anyway."

"Running away? Great." David stood in the doorway.

"What's it to you? I'd think you'd be happy to have such a stupid person out of your way."

"Trish, David." Marge raised her voice.

"I'm going, and that's it!" Trish snapped the locks on the suitcase.

Marge rose to her feet. "Enough!" The word sliced the air.

Trish and David stared at their mother.

Marge took a deep breath. "Now . . ." She looked to Trish, then David. "I know you mean well, David, but you're not helping things right now. Let me deal with your sister."

"Right." David turned and retreated down the hall.

"Trish, I don't want you to go to Kentucky right now. Running away never solved anything."

You should know, Trish thought, glaring at her mother. *You checked out when things got too tough, remember?* But nothing came out of her mouth; she just gritted her teeth. Then, "Mom, I'll be back in time for school, I promise. Maybe this trip will help me. It can't hurt anything."

Marge pulled the desk chair out and sat with her arms resting on its back. She took a deep breath and sighed, watching Trish pace from the bed to the window.

Trish sank down on the end of the bed. "Mom, I feel like I'm going crazy. What am I going to do? What's happening to me? To us?" Her voice faded into a whisper.

Marge shook her head, then rested her chin on her rolled fists. "It's called grief, Trish. We all have to work through it." She looked out the window, seeming to study the leaves rustling in the slight breeze. Then she smiled at Trish, as if returning from a faraway place. "I know how much you love that horse. Maybe seeing him *would* help. But I have one condition . . ." She paused. ". . . that you go see Pastor Mort first."

Trish fell back across the bed. "I can't, Mom. I just can't. Not now, anyway. I—I'll go when I get back." She chewed on her thumbnail. "Please don't make me go. Not now."

"What about Patrick's training schedule?"

"David can ride for the four, five days I'm gone."

Marge pushed her hair off her forehead. "You promise you'll see Pastor Mort when you get back?"

Trish nodded. "Yes. I will. I really will."

"Call the Shipsons, then, and ask if it's all right with them."

"Thanks, Mom!"

CHAPTER 9

Trish wondered if Spitfire would look different.

She stared out the plane window as the aircraft approached the Lexington Airport. She still had a hard time believing she was in Kentucky. Only yesterday she'd had the incident with Miss Tee on the road. It seemed as if her telescope were playing tricks on her, putting home at the small end, far away.

She'd called Rhonda last night to say she was leaving for a few days. It was strange, but she hadn't told her best friend about the fight, if you could call it that, with her mother and her brother. Was she losing contact with Rhonda too?

Mrs. Shipson had promised to meet the plane, even seemed offended when Trish talked about renting a car.

Trish chewed on her knuckle. She hadn't called Red. Did she want to see him too? Why were there so many questions buzzing around in her head? She wished things could go back to the way they used to be.

Bernice Shipson, silver-haired, and stylish as ever, greeted Trish with a quick hug. Her soft accent was musical and friendly. "Do you have other luggage to pick up?"

"Yes, I couldn't fit it all into my carry-on." Trish dug out her tickets to show the baggage claim. "I really appreciate your letting me come on such short notice."

"We meant it when we said you are welcome anytime, Trish. I found myself feeling a little jealous when Martha Finley talked about you going to California. We haven't had young people in our home for a long while."

"I don't remember hearing you speak of children." Trish switched her bag from one shoulder to the other.

"No, our only son was killed in Viet Nam," Mrs. Shipson said softly.

"Oh . . . I—I'm so sorry," Trish stammered. "I didn't know."

"Not many people do. It was a long time ago. The pain has eased considerably . . ." She smiled at Trish. "That's why I can tell you with all honesty that you will get through this time of grief for your father. Right now it hurts so badly you don't know how you'll ever make it, but God lives up to His promises. Someday the pain will be bittersweet—blended with all the good memories."

It was hard for Trish to hear this. *Wasn't it God who had let her father die?*

As if reading her mind, Mrs. Shipson laid her hand on Trish's arm. "Right now you are so angry with God, you're certain you'll never have anything to do with Him again."

Trish stared at her. "You felt that way, too?"

The woman nodded.

"What did you do?"

"I decided to trust God—and rest. There was nothing else I could do."

A hurrying traveler bumped into Trish and apologized.

"We'll talk again, if you like. I just wanted you to

know that I understand what you're feeling. And I'm glad Donald and I could be here for you." She smiled through misty eyes. "Now, let's get your things. A certain black horse will be thrilled to see you."

As they were loading Trish's bags in the trunk, Trish said, "Mrs. Shipson . . ."

"Please call me Bernice."

"Bernice, thank you."

Conversation flowed between them all the way to BlueMist Farms as though they were old friends. Bernice pointed out the sights and shared bits of local folklore.

Trish felt as if she were in a whole new world. Even the soft leather seat of the Cadillac they were riding in seemed to wrap comfort around her. And the gentle, cool air blowing through the air vents refreshed her. *If only Dad were here, it would be perfect* flitted through her mind. *If only there were no more if only's.* She tried to concentrate on the story Bernice was telling her.

They drove straight down to the stallion barn. Trish whistled her two-tone call to Spitfire as soon as she stepped out of the car. A sharp whinny and pounding hooves was her immediate answer. Inside the barn, Spitfire waited impatiently at the door of his stall. He nickered again and then again, as though he couldn't believe what he was seeing.

Trish leaned her forehead against his and rubbed both his satiny cheeks with trembling hands. "I've missed you so, fella; you just have no idea."

He bumped her gently with his nose and nuzzled her pocket. Trish pulled out a withered bit of carrot, but Spitfire didn't seem to mind. He munched once and blew in her face, ruffling her bangs. Trish rubbed his ears and smoothed his forelock.

"I think he missed you as much as you missed him." Bernice stood back to let the two of them talk.

"I see you made it, lass." Timmy O'Ryan sounded so much like Patrick that Trish did a double take. "Like I told you on the phone, he was off his feed for a few days at first. Kind of moped around here, but I can see you're the medicine he needed."

"And you for me," Trish murmured into the colt's twitching ears. Spitfire shook his head. Her breath tickled. He draped his head over her shoulder, cocked a back foot, and sighed. His eyes closed in contentment as Trish kept stroking.

Timmy laughed, a low, musical chuckle. "What a baby he is. One of the grooms wouldn't believe this unless he saw it."

"Why, did something happen?"

"Spitfire was living up to his name one morning. Jumping around and backing his groom into a corner. Then he grabbed the guy's hat and threw it across the stall." The trainer rocked back on his heels. "You can be sure that Nick is real cautious around the big black now."

"Up to your old tricks, eh?" Trish jiggled Spitfire's halter to wake him up. "Hats are his favorite toy. I think he just likes to see how people react. Huh, fella?" Trish tickled the colt's whiskery upper lip.

Spitfire twitched it back and forth and licked her hand.

"Why don't you exercise him every morning while you're here," Timmy said, a grin creasing his leathery face.

"I'd love to." Trish smoothed one hand after the other down the black's long face.

"Dinner's waiting up at the house," Mrs. Shipson

92

said, after checking her watch. "If you can bear to leave him, that is."

Trish gave Spitfire a last pat. "See you in the morning, fella." The colt nickered when she walked away, then let loose with a shrill whinny. "I'll be back." Trish waved from the door.

"There's no doubt he's your horse," Bernice said as she slid into the driver's side of the car.

"Yeah, I know."

At the house, Mrs. Shipson led Trish down the hall to the same lovely, antique-furnished room. "I've been calling this Trish's room ever since you were here," she said. The sheer curtains billowed in the evening breeze as she opened the door. "I hate to rush you, but dinner is ready to serve. Just wash and come down. You can put your things away later, if that's all right."

"Sure. I'll be right down."

The same friendly woman served dinner as before. "Now, y'all just eat up," she said with a broad smile. "There's nothing like my cookin' out your way." She set a platter of fried chicken right in front of Trish. "Now, that there's fried okra, in case you ain't had that before." She pointed to a bowl of unfamiliar green vegetable. "And I 'spect you to have more'n one biscuit. We gotta spoil you right quick if you're gonna stay only four days." Her laugh drifted back over her shoulder as she returned to the kitchen for more food.

Mr. Shipson said the blessing and then smiled at Trish. "Sarah's one of a kind. She and I grew up together. Her mother was our family cook before her. And you'd better eat her food or her feelings will be hurt. There's nothing she likes better than seeing people enjoy her cooking."

Trish took a piece of chicken and passed the platter to Bernice. "She made enough to feed ten teenagers."

"I know. She's always afraid someone will go away hungry."

Not much chance of that, Trish thought as she turned down a third helping. She felt she would burst.

"I thought we might go to Louisville tomorrow to attend the races," Bernice said, tucking her snowy-white napkin back into the silver napkin ring. "I've heard a certain red-headed jockey is riding tomorrow."

Trish could feel the heat of a blush rise to her cheeks. She grinned at the older woman. "I'd like that."

"Does he know you're here?"

Trish shook her head.

"Then we'll just surprise him, won't we?"

The ride around the track the next morning was a bit of heaven for Trish. She rode Spitfire around several times, and then Timmy beckoned her off to a utility track that led toward a grove of trees.

Trish inhaled deeply of the soft morning air. The sun just peeked over the tops of the lacy-leaved oak trees, gilding everything with a golden brush. Spitfire snorted and jigged sideways. The bit jangled as he tossed his head.

"They fox hunt through here in the fall," Timmy said as they jogged along. "You should come for that sometime. You know how to jump?"

"Not really, although I've tried it a couple of times. My best friend is the jumper in the bunch. She'd go crazy here."

"Bring her along. I'm sure we could find mounts for both of you. You're planning on coming for the Breeder's Cup anyway, aren't you?"

A thrill of excitement skittered up Trish's back. "Uh
. . . I don't know yet." *Wouldn't that be something. But I'd
have to be back in school in October.* It was an idea worth
thinking about, anyway.

Driving into the parking lot at Churchill Downs the
next afternoon brought back a rush of memories for
Trish. But being a spectator instead of a jockey made it
easier as she leaned on the outside of the fence to the
paddocks.

"Hey, Red, good luck!" Trish called after him as he
followed the others to the saddling paddock.

Red stopped so fast the jockey behind him bumped
into him.

"Trish!" He stepped toward her, a grin splitting his
face. He clasped her cheeks in both hands and planted a
kiss right on her astonished mouth. "I can't believe
you're here. Why didn't you call? I could have met your
plane."

"I know. So, I surprised you." Trish wasn't sure if her
cheeks were warm from a blush or from his hands.

"See you right after this race, okay?" Red waved at
the official who motioned him to the saddling paddock.
"Don't you leave, hear?" He blew her another kiss as he
backpedaled to the paddock.

"I think that young man is very fond of you." Bernice
chuckled softly. "His face just lit up when you called his
name."

Trish fanned herself with the program. *Talk about
faces lighting up.*

"Would you like something to drink before we head
for our box?"

"Thank you. That would be nice."

After another delicious meal in the evening, Trish thought, *I could get used to this lifestyle. A private box at the track, someone to wait on me, make my bed. I get to play with Spitfire, and no mucking stalls.*

Up in her room, she leaned back against the stack of lace-trimmed pillows on her bed. *Yes, I could like this.* Home seemed very far away—like on another planet. Thoughts of Red pulled her ahead to the next afternoon. He planned to take her out to dinner and to a movie. Mrs. Shipson had winked and nodded her approval when she heard of the invitation.

After their ride the next morning, Spitfire nibbled Trish's braid as she brushed him. "Knock it off." Trish smacked him on the nose, then hugged him. "You big goof; when are you gonna grow up?" Spitfire snorted and shook his head.

"I think he understands every word you say," Donald Shipson said as he watched the girl and horse together.

"I was the first human to touch him." Trish brushed a bit of straw off the colt's ear. "We've been best buds ever since."

"Must be terribly hard for you at home, with both him and your father gone."

Trish nodded. "It is."

"Well, if you ever decide to come to Kentucky, you know where your home is." He pushed away from the stall door. "You about ready for breakfast?"

"You people eat like this all the time?"

"You have to learn to pick and choose—and not let Sarah railroad you. Also, I run from the big house to the barns rather than take a car. That helps."

Together, they jogged down the road and across the creek. Huge oak trees shaded the drive to the house and made the rise deceptive. Trish was puffing a bit when they stopped at the front porch.

————

The date with Red would live on in Trish's memory for a long time. He took her to a white-tablecloth restaurant, where she wished she'd had a nice dress to wear instead of just slacks and a blouse. She tried cajun food for the first time and nearly choked on the spicy blackened red fish.

Red handed her the bread basket. "Here. This works better than water." His eyes twinkled in the candlelight.

After the dessert, which the waiter brought flaming to their table, Red set a small box in front of Trish. "So you think of me often," he said softly.

"I already do." Trish fingered the gold cross he'd given her before. "I wear it all the time."

Her hand trembled as she opened the box. Inside lay a gold link bracelet with a delicate gold charm. It was a racing horse and jockey. "Oh, Red, it's beautiful!" She lifted it from the box and looked at it more closely. "Thank you," she said to his smiling face. It was all she could manage. The familiar lump had taken up its place in her throat.

Red put the bracelet on Trish's wrist and fastened the clasp and the safety chain. "Now you can think of me *more* often." He leaned forward and kissed her softly.

————

Before she knew it, Sunday arrived—time to go home. Red, the Shipsons, and Timmy O'Ryan waved her off at the airport. Trish could feel a smile deep inside as she sat on the plane waiting for take-off. If this had been a true example of southern hospitality, she knew she liked it.

Her mood lasted until the plane landed in Portland. Marge and David were there to meet her, but she still looked for her father. All the pain came crashing down around her. He would never again be there to welcome her home.

CHAPTER 10

Anywhere is better than home, Trish thought.

She stared at the empty recliner by the fireplace. It was always the first place she looked when she came in the front door—as if the last weeks had been a bad dream.

The weight of her loss settled heavier on her shoulders with each step down the hall to her bedroom. She dropped her suitcase, threw herself across her bed, and drifted off into that no-man's-land between waking and sleeping.

Sometime later she jerked upright. "Dad?" She stared around the room, her gaze searching for the source of the voice. She was so certain she'd heard her father call her. But there was no one there. She could only hear the drone of the television from the living room.

She rubbed her eyes and shook her head. Was she really going crazy after all? When she flopped back against the pillows, scenes of Kentucky drifted through her mind. Spitfire, the dates with Red, BlueMist Farms and the wonderful people there. Why did the pain return when she came home?

"I can't stand this," she muttered as she pulled on her boots. She ran down the hall and out the front door, totally ignoring her mother's questioning voice.

"Where you going?" David asked as she stormed into the tack room. He dropped the bridle he'd been cleaning and rose to his feet. Patrick looked up from the records he'd been studying.

"Welcome home, lass." He shut the book. "Can we be helpin' you?"

"No." Trish reached for bridle and saddle. "I'm just going riding for a while on Dan'l. I won't be gone long."

"It's getting late to be out on the road."

"I know. I'll go back up the hill."

"You okay, Trish?" David sat back down.

"I guess." But she shook her head as she said it.

Dan'l seemed to enjoy the ride more than Trish did. He danced back into the stable area and tossed his head when she jumped to the ground. "Thanks, old man." Trish stripped off the tack and gave the aging gray thoroughbred a halfhearted brushing before she released him back into pasture.

The lights from Patrick's mobile home brightened the road up to the house. "I should stop and see him," she told Caesar as they padded up the gentle rise. "Maybe tomorrow."

She stopped for a moment on the deck at the back of the house. Her mother's fuchsias and begonias spilled over their baskets in explosions of pinks and purples. Peeper frogs chorused from down by the drainage ditch. Trish and her father used to sit out here and watch the hummingbirds drink at the purple and white fuchsia blossoms.

Memories everywhere.

She slid open the sliding glass door into the family room. The fish tank bubbled away in the corner, just like always.

"There's dinner in the oven," her mother called from the living room. Trish could hear the squeak of her mother's rocker. She must be knitting—like always.

"Thanks, anyway, I'm not hung—" Trish froze in the doorway. "What are you doing in Dad's chair?" Her voice cracked on the words.

David looked up from his place in the worn leather recliner. "What's with you?"

"That's Dad's chair. You have no right sitting there." She advanced on him like she would pull him bodily from the chair.

"Knock it off. I can sit here; Dad wouldn't mind." David raised his hands to keep her from pounding him.

"Trish, what is the matter with you?" Marge rose from her rocker.

"That's Dad chair!" Trish screamed. "Neither of you care!" She stormed from the room, but before she was out of earshot she heard David say, "You'd better do something about her, Mom, before she goes off the deep end."

Trish entered the sanctuary of her own room, wrapped both arms around herself to stop the shaking. Her throat and eyes burned. Was this what life would be like at home from now on? She bit her lip hard. *Who needs this?*

It sounded as if her mother were in the next county when she came into Trish's room sometime later. "Trish, we need to talk about this."

Trish buried her face deeper in the pillow and shook her head. "I can't," she mumbled. She fell back into that black hole where memories and bad feelings didn't exist.

She missed morning works the next day, and slept until her mother came in at ten. "You have to register today, Trish." The voice cut through Trish's fog like a drill sergeant's.

Trish rolled on her back and threw an arm over her face. "I have all day."

"No, you have an appointment with Pastor Mort at one. And you need to register first."

Trish threw back the covers and leaped to her feet. "I'm not talking to him today, Mom."

"Yes, you are," Marge said firmly. "You promised me you would when you got back from Kentucky, remember?"

"Fine. I need to go to the bathroom." She brushed past her mother and headed down the hall. Her head pounded like a herd of runaway ponies.

She drove into Vancouver with the top of the convertible down even though the skies were gray. Maybe a little rain on her head wouldn't hurt. *You gotta get hold of yourself*, she ordered. *You're acting crazy.*

She stopped at a stoplight. Then the sound of a horn behind her made her pop the clutch. The car stalled. Another horn blared while Trish restarted her car and eased through the signal. She'd zoned out again.

A light mist was falling as Trish turned into the parking lot of the administration building at Clark College. She pushed the button to raise the convertible top and waited till it snapped in place. Raindrops formed a trickle down the windshield. Even the sky was crying. She clamped down on the thought.

She finally pushed herself out of the car and headed for the double glass doors. She could see long tables set up for registration inside.

"Excuse me," someone behind her said.

Trish still had her hand on the door. She removed it

and stepped aside. She couldn't make herself go in.

She arrived early at the church for her appointment. When she closed her eyes and rested her head against the neck rest in her car, she tried to picture Spitfire—and their rides in Kentucky. The picture wouldn't come. All she could see was the misery on her mother's face, and on David's when she yelled at him. What was she doing to them?

A tap on her window brought her back to the present with a start. "Oh—Pastor Mort."

"Sorry, Trish. I didn't mean to startle you. Would you like to come in now?"

Trish nodded and bit back the *Not really*.

"That's some car you have there. We missed you. How was Kentucky?"

"Oh, it was . . . wonderful. Spitfire was as happy to see me as I was to see him. It's hard being so far apart." She walked through the door he held open for her. "Thanks."

"Can I get you a Coke or something?" Pastor Mort hung his coat on a rack by the door.

Trish shook her head. "No, thanks."

"Sit down, sit down. I know this is hard for you, Trish, but I'm glad to see you. It seems like you've been gone a long time." He took a chair opposite Trish, rather than behind his desk.

Trish crossed her arms over her chest and slid down a bit in her chair. "I really have nothing to say." She tried to sound casual, but realized she sounded rude.

"Your mother's concerned about you, Trish."

"Yeah, I know."

"Did you get registered at the college?"

Trish shook her head. "I couldn't."

"No room in the class?"

She shook her head again. "No, that wasn't it. I just couldn't do it."

"I see." He tapped a finger against his chin and leaned forward. "Trish, I want to help you, and I know I can, but you have to want help. I'm here for you anytime—day or night. I'll come to your house, if that would be easier for you." He waited for her response.

"I . . . ah—" Trish bit her bottom lip. "Okay, that would be easier." She stood, and fled from the room before the pastor could say anything more.

I just had to get outta there, she thought on the drive home. *Maybe I need to get out of here!*

"So what time is your class?" Marge asked from her rocking chair when Trish came in.

"No class." Trish started down the hall to her room.

"You mean they were full already?"

Trish leaned her forehead on her crossed arms against the wall. "No, I mean I didn't register. Mom, I can't even think. I zone out, fall asleep. I just can't take chemistry now; I'd flunk for sure."

"Did you talk to Pastor Mort?"

"I saw him. We talked a little."

"Trish, you *will* see him again? You promised."

"Yes, Mother. I will see him again. He's going to come to the house."

"Okay. I've backed off long enough, and I feel it's time you get some help. You've been rude, and even cruel—to all of us. I won't tolerate it any longer. Your dad and I did not raise you to act like this."

"Mom— You think I *like* what's happened to us?" Trish hurled the words at her mother. "You can't just put a Band-Aid on it and expect everything to be all right.

What can Pastor Mort do? What can anyone do? You . . . you just don't understand." She whirled in the hall and marched out the front door.

Jumping into her car, she jammed the key into the ignition and cranked it hard. The engine roared to life. She threw it into first, and gravel spun from the tires as she roared out the driveway.

After shifting into third out on the road, Trish floored it. The car leaped forward, picking up speed—forty, fifty, sixty. She cranked the wheel hard around the first curve.

Was she trying to outrun the voices screaming in her head? Seventy. Trish hit the brakes to make it around a ninety-degree bend. Her front wheels hit the shoulder but she jerked the car back on course.

For a few minutes she drove more cautiously, her heart pounding. She flicked on the radio to drown out her thoughts.

Radio blaring, she picked up speed again. The mist was coming steadily now, and she turned on the wipers.

Up into the Hockinson Hills, Trish followed the winding road. Driving like this was like racing a thoroughbred, the car responsive to the wheel like a horse to the bit. She swung a hard left. The car skidded. Trish caught it and gritted her teeth until she straightened again.

Another hard right. She tapped the breaks. A hard left. Too soon! She slammed on her brakes and left the road, bumping over ruts and into a hayfield. Her head hit the roof. Slamming down again she bit her tongue.

The car stalled on a hay bale.

Trish leaned her head on the steering wheel. She felt like throwing up. Her hands shook so hard she could hardly turn off the ignition. She threw open the door in time to lose whatever was in her stomach.

Her dad was gone. Spitfire was gone. And now she'd wrecked her car. What else was left? Maybe she should have hit that tree.

Then it all would have been over.

CHAPTER 11

But it wasn't over.

Trish dug in her purse for a tissue and wiped her mouth. "Oh, for a drink of water," she whispered in the stillness. When she finally felt like her legs would hold her up, she opened the door and stepped out. Walking around the car, she checked for damage. The only problem she could see was a flat tire on the front passenger side.

She got back in and turned the key. The engine started immediately, and Trish levered the gearshift gently into reverse. Slowly, she eased out the clutch and backed the car off the hay bale.

"Too bad you weren't equipped with a phone too," she said, patting the dashboard. "I don't see a house anywhere." She'd shut the engine off again, and her voice seemed to echo in the quietness around her.

"Well, if anyone is going to change that tire, it's going to have to be me." At least she had the tools and knew how to use them. Somehow, though, she'd never quite planned on changing a tire in the rain, at dusk, and in a hayfield—on her new car.

What is your mother going to say now? Nagger piped up.

"Plenty, I suppose," Trish answered curtly.

When she got back on to the road she noticed the alignment was off; it was hard to steer and keep the car on the road. Trish felt like crawling into the house. There was no way to hide the fact that she'd had some trouble. She was soaked, and her clothes were dirty.

"What happened to you?" Marge gasped.

Trish tried to sound casual. "I missed a curve and ended up on a hay bale. A front tire went flat, so I changed it."

"Where were you?"

"Somewhere up in the Hockinson Hills."

"Tricia Evanston, you scared me half to death when you took off like you did. And look at you."

"Are you hurt, lass?" Trish could hear disappointment in Patrick's voice.

"Not really. Something's wrong with the car, though."

David shook his head. "Nice going, Trish."

"I think we need to talk." Trish sighed. "Let me go to the bathroom first and get cleaned up. I need something to drink, too. My stomach hurts."

Marge followed her daughter to the bathroom. "Let me see your mouth. Is it bleeding?"

"I just bit my tongue." Trish stuck it out for inspection. She rinsed her mouth and wiped off her face. "Really, I'm okay. Just shook up." Her hands trembled as she dried them.

Marge pulled Trish into her arms. "Oh, Tee, if anything happened to you, I don't know what I'd do."

Trish leaned limply against her mother. She'd held the tears in so long they wouldn't come even when she wanted them to. Her throat and eyes burned as she and Marge walked back to the kitchen.

Trish slumped into her chair at the big oak table.

Lifting her head to look at her mother took a major effort.

"I think you bent the tie rods in the front end of your car," David announced, washing his hands at the kitchen sink. "I couldn't see any leaking from the radiator or the oil pan, though. You'll have to take it in to the garage in the morning."

"I guessed that, David."

"I think you ruined the tire, too."

"What did you want to talk about, Trish?" Marge asked, stopping David's recital of damages.

"I need to get back to racing." Trish looked at her mother imploringly. "I'll go crazy unless I get busy again. Everywhere I look I expect to see Dad—"

"Don't you think the rest of us feel the same way?" David asked accusingly. "You're not the only—"

"David . . ." Marge cut him off.

"I know." Trish ran her fingers along the edge of the table runner.

"What about the chemistry makeup?" Marge asked.

"Adam said there are several colleges near where I'd be staying in California. I can take classes at night, or hire a tutor if I have to. Mom, please let me go."

The silence at the table stretched into minutes. The fish tank bubbled in the corner; Caesar thumped his leg on the deck as he scratched for fleas.

Trish looked up to see her mother with her eyes closed, her hand propping up her forehead. Trish knew her mother was probably praying.

She didn't dare look at her brother. She knew she wouldn't get any sympathy from him.

Marge finally dropped her hand and looked at her daughter. "I have one condition and there will be no arguing it. If you want to go to California, you will have to talk with Pastor Mort first. No games."

Trish swallowed hard. "Okay. I can do that."

David shook his head, and Marge laid her hand on his arm to keep him from leaving the table.

"And you'll be back in time for school, whether the season is finished there or not. There will be no discussion about that, either."

Trish nodded. School seemed a long way off.

Patrick had stepped into the room when Marge mentioned California. She asked him, "How quickly can you make the necessary arrangements?"

"A couple of days. The horses are ready any time. I'll call Adam and get a horse hauler." He looked to David. "Who do you generally use?"

"We borrowed Diego's van last winter. I could call him and see about using it again. He may have a horse or two he wants to send down there, too."

"How many does the van hold?"

"Six, I think."

Trish thought she'd be relieved if her mother agreed to her wishes, but instead she felt drained. She pushed her chair back and stood up. "Thanks, Mom. We'll talk more tomorrow." She tried to catch David's eye but he wouldn't look at her.

Once in bed, her Nagger began to taunt her. *You used to trust God and His promises . . . the verses that were on your wall. Your life would be a lot easier if . . .* Trish groaned and turned over, burying her head under the pillow.

After working the horses in the morning, Trish called the Chrysler dealership and made an appointment to bring in her car.

"Mom, would you follow me into the shop?" Trish asked after she'd hung up the phone.

"Sure." Marge leaned against the sink, sipping hot coffee. "What time?"

"Right away. I just need to change clothes."

Trish brushed her hair in front of the bathroom mirror. She didn't think she looked like herself. Even her hair was unmanageable. The charm from her new bracelet clinked against the edge of the sink when she leaned over to brush her teeth. "Whoa, I haven't called Red in a while—or written him."

After her car was looked over, Trish sat in a state of shock. The estimate on the repairs read between $2,500 and $3,000. New bumper, repair tie rods, adjust alignment, replace dented oil pan—and that was only what could be readily seen. There could be more damage inside.

The only good news was that she should be able to pick the car up the next evening.

"Are you going to file an insurance claim?" her mother asked as they walked back to the family station wagon.

"I don't know. What do you think?" Trish rubbed her forehead with the tips of her fingers. She winced as she hit a tender spot. She must have banged her head on the steering wheel.

"It might be better to pay it off yourself, since the accident was your fault. That way it won't show up on your record. Your insurance rate could go up quite a bit at your age."

"I'll have to get money transferred from savings to checking, then. Can we stop by the bank?"

Marge nodded as she pulled out onto the street.

"When will you see Pastor Mort?"

She'd decided to see him at his office. "I'm going in this afternoon at three. Can I borrow your car?" Trish hated to ask, but she had no choice.

Sitting in the pastor's office, Trish felt like a child being reprimanded in the principal's office at school.

"Who are you mad at, Trish?" Pastor Mort said gently after a few moments of general conversation.

Trish shrugged. "No one, I guess."

"Do you think that drive you took was because of anger?"

Trish tightened her jaw. "Maybe." If she didn't talk much, maybe this would be over sooner than she thought. At least she was doing what her mother had asked.

"I think you're mad at yourself."

Trish raised her eyebrows. "Maybe. I know driving like I did was stupid. I'll never do that again." Her voice became stronger. "Actually, I can't believe I did it. Three thousand dollars—maybe more."

"Do you think you could be mad at your dad for dying?"

"That too . . ." Her voice trailed off.

"How about God?"

Trish nodded. How did he know all this stuff? "My dad used to say that God heals. He had me memorize Bible verses about it." Trish shoved herself to her feet. "Yes, I'd say I was mad at God. He doesn't live up to His promises . . ." Her voice broke. "I don't want to hear about God's promises ever again."

Pastor Mort just nodded.

Trish sat down again. "What's worse—my mother is taking over Dad's place! And my brother sits in Dad's chair. Patrick's doing his work down at the barns. No one seems to miss him except me. Why did he leave me?"

"I don't think your father wanted to leave you, Trish, and I understand how you feel."

"Do you?" Trish glared at him. "You talk about how God is so good. Well, I don't see Him that way." Trish held her head in her hands. She felt like a volcano about to erupt.

She pulled her legs up underneath her. "I'm sorry—"

"It's okay." Pastor Mort poured her a glass of water from the pitcher on his desk. "Is there anything else you want to say?"

"That's not enough?" She sipped the water.

"No, I think there's more."

Trish stared into her glass. "I guess I—uh—I feel so . . . guilty. Like it's my fault that Dad died. And that I shouldn't be mad like this. Sometimes I just want to die . . . it hurts so bad." She leaned her head against the back of the chair.

"Do you know anything about the grieving process, Trish?"

Trish shrugged. "I—I guess you're sad, and you cry a lot."

"Have you cried a lot?"

"At first I did. Mostly when I was alone. Now I can't. There aren't any more tears, I guess."

"You've locked them away, Trish. There are more tears, and you should let them come. Grief comes in stages. Denial, anger, fear, guilt—it's all normal. Every person that suffers a loss experiences these stages of grief—in different degrees, of course. Sometimes we go back and forth between emotions. It's okay to be angry at God, by the way. He loves you no matter what you think of Him."

Trish muttered into her glass, "If this is love, what is hate like?"

"God isn't punishing you or trying to hurt you, Trish. We can't always know *why* or understand what life throws at us. As long as we live on the earth there is going to be some pain, illness, death. God only promises to get us through it—if we trust Him. You have to deal with your feelings. They aren't good or bad, they're just there—a part of you. By trying to lock them up, not allowing yourself to cry, you get stuck in the rage. Tears are healing, Trish. They are not a sign of weakness."

"Do you think I drove off like I did because I was stuck in a rage?"

"What do you think?"

Trish nodded in spite of herself. "But nothing will bring my dad back. And I can't live without him."

"It may seem like that right now. But you have to give it some time. You can't be over your grief so quickly. You know your dad would want you to go on and enjoy your life. He did the best he could with his. I have a suggestion. How about writing a letter to God, telling Him exactly how you feel? Don't hold anything back; tell it like it is. And then write a letter to your father."

Trish stared at the pastor, as if he were a little wacky.

"Your dad found writing in his journal was a big help back in the early days of his illness, when he was angry and scared."

"He was angry and scared?"

"Yes, he was. He and I did a lot of talking when he was in the hospital that first time. He said journaling helped a lot. He could say what he felt without feeling like he was being judged."

"I don't see how writing can help."

"I agree it doesn't make much sense at first, but try it. It works. Will you try, Trish?"

"I—I'll see. Maybe I will."

"Let me know when you do, and what you think of it."

Trish stood to her feet. "Is that all?"

"I think that will do for now. Thanks for coming, Trish."

Why is he thanking me? "Thank you."

Once outside, Trish felt free as a swallow in the spring. Maybe it was just the fresh air. She remembered her father suggesting journaling to her. And whether she wanted to admit it or not, talking to Pastor Mort *did* make her feel better.

At home, David greeted her with, "Patrick thinks Miss Tee may have torn a ligament in her shoulder—because of that run on the road."

CHAPTER 12

Gatesby didn't want to leave home.

"Do you always have to be a jerk?" Trish muttered as she clamped her hands tighter on the lead shank. Her shoulder already ached from the force of the gelding's high jinks.

"Walk him around and we'll try again." Patrick planted both hands on his hips. "Sure and he can be an ornery beast."

"You got that right." David glared at his charge. "Okay, Trish, let's take him around again and then right up the ramp without slowing or stopping."

This time Gatesby walked in without a snort. David kept up his muttering while tying the horse in place. "Anderson didn't do us any favors when he brought you back."

Gatesby nosed David's gloved hand. "Knock it off."

"You really gotta watch him when he does that," Trish told Patrick. The bay swung his hindquarters and trapped David in the stall.

"Move over, you miserable hunk of horse," David ordered, slapping Gatesby's shoulder. The horse squeezed him tighter. "Trish!"

"It's good to know I'm needed," she said sweetly. "All right, Gatesby, get over." The gelding straightened out and peered over his shoulder. Trish slipped in beside him and fed him a carrot piece from her pocket. "You really are a pain, you know." She rubbed his forehead and smoothed the forelock in place. "Now, you behave yourself."

The two fillies walked in with no problems. The men closed the doors and they were ready to roll. David and Patrick would take turns driving the van, and Trish would follow in her car.

"Please be careful," Marge cautioned as she handed a small cooler to the men and another to Trish. "Call me as soon as you get there." She leaned in the window to kiss Trish on the cheek. "I'll be praying for you."

"Don't worry, Mom. Okay?"

"You know I don't worry anymore." A smile flitted across her face and disappeared. For a long time worrying had been a serious problem for Marge, but now it had become a family joke. "It's not easy letting my sixteen-year-old daughter go off like this, though."

"The Finleys are probably more protective than you are," Trish said. "I'll call often."

"Maybe even write?"

"Maybe." Trish waved as she followed the silver van down the driveway.

The trip was uneventful, but long, because they had decided to drive straight through. They pulled into the backside of Bay Meadows at ten in the evening. The guard at the gate gave them instructions to Finleys' barn.

"Any trouble?" Adam asked as they stepped down from the cab.

"None." David arched his back and dug his fists into the tight muscles.

Trish got out and stretched, too. She bent from side

to side and rotated her shoulders, then stepped easily into Adam Finley's embrace. "It's good to see you. That was a long haul; I'll take the plane anytime."

"Glad you could come, Trish."

"How are you, Adam?" Patrick asked. "Your barn looks real good."

"I'm doing good, and thanks. The vet will be down here right away to check your horses in. I called him as soon as the gate let me know you were here. So—four new horses in my care. Sure you don't want to stay and help me out, Patrick?"

Patrick shook his head. "Sorry, too much to do up north."

"You miss the track?"

Trish had never really thought about the fact that Patrick might miss the track. She waited for his answer. What if Patrick didn't want to stay with them at Runnin' On Farm?

"Oh, some, yes. But it won't be long before Portland opens. Time flies awful fast when you're having fun." Patrick tipped his hat back on his head. "Gotta keep up with these young folks here."

Trish breathed a sigh of relief. They really did need Patrick now that Dad was gone.

It didn't take long for the vet to check the animals for signs of fever or other illness. As soon as he finished drawing blood samples, they led the horses into their new stalls.

"You'll have plenty to keep you busy here," Patrick said to Trish as they hooked the last gate. "You'll be switching mounts right quick in the mornings."

"At least I don't have to clean stalls." She smiled.

"Yeah, like you've been overworked in that department lately." The sarcasm in David's voice touched a nerve in Trish. Obviously, he still wasn't pleased about her leaving home for the summer.

She missed the easy teamwork with her brother. Was that gone for good too?

"I made reservations for you at a motel across the street," Adam said to the two men. "You can park the van in the lot and I'll give you a ride over. Trish, your room is ready at our condominium. Martha can't wait to see you."

"See you in the morning," Trish called as she waved good-night to David and Patrick.

Trish tried to memorize their route as she followed Adam to his home. He said they had a little condominium, but when he showed her the program numbers on the entry gate she began to wonder.

After winding up a narrow road, he parked in front of a three-level home, stair-stepped into the hill. Martha Finley stood waving from a huge bay window on the second floor. The cream stucco building with a Spanish-tile roof made her think of the Finley ranch in the San Joaquin Valley.

Martha met them at the ornately carved oak door. Black wrought-iron railings flanked the stairs. "My dear, you have no idea how happy I am to see you!" She hugged Trish and ushered her into the tiled entry. Stairs led up and down to the other levels, and to the right Trish could see the lights of San Mateo with the black hole of San Francisco Bay beyond.

"Wow!" Trish walked across the plush cream carpet to stand in front of the window. She could see the blinking lights of two planes on their slanting approach to San Francisco International Airport. "What a view!"

"We like it." Martha stood beside her. "Being up high like this makes city living bearable. We'd both rather be at the ranch, but this is where the tracks are. If you look off to the left, you can see the San Francisco skyline. I hope you like it here."

"I'm sure I will. Thank you for having me."

"It's our pleasure, dear. Adam teases me about needing someone to fuss over. Come on, I'll show you to your room. It's upstairs; I thought you'd like the view." She pointed to pictures of their three sons and families as they climbed the stairs.

Trish's room faced south. Martha opened the teal-blue drapes to show her the private deck.

Trish dropped her bag on the pile carpet of blues and greens. "What a beautiful room, Martha."

"It did turn out rather nicely, didn't it?"

"Is it new?"

"Yes. This was one of the boys' rooms. When I thought you might be coming to visit us, I redecorated it. You have your own bathroom; there are fresh towels. Now, is there anything else you need out of your car tonight? Are you hungry or thirsty?"

Trish shook her head. "No, I have all I need. And thanks, I'm just fine."

"Good-night then, Trish. We'll see you in the morning."

Trish sank down onto the queen-sized bed and stifled a huge yawn. Morning would be here soon. . . .

"Yes?" she answered a tap on the door.

"You can sleep in tomorrow if you'd like." It was Adam. "I know you're beat from that long trip."

"I'll be ready when you are. What time do you leave?"

"Four-thirty." He chuckled.

Trish glanced at the clock. It was midnight. "See you then."

———

Trish slept well and awoke surprisingly refreshed. Her car was blanketed in fog when she stepped into it. She was mounted on Firefly and out on the track just as a tinge of pink cracked the eastern sky. One of Finley's regular exercise riders rode beside her.

"This is the training track; they're working on the main track behind us." Sam clucked her horse into a trot.

Trish did the same. Firefly settled into her easy gait, alert to every sight and sound on the new track.

"How's it feel to be a Triple Crown winner?" Sam pulled her mount to a walk.

"I don't know. It's like it all happened a long time ago—to someone else." Trish smoothed the filly's mane to one side. "So much has gone on since then."

"Yeah, I heard about your dad. What a bummer." She looked over at Trish. "We were all real sorry to hear it."

"Thanks." Trish didn't know what else to say. "Ahhh . . . you been riding long?"

"This is my third year. Adam says he'll let me race this season. I had some mounts on the fair circuit last year. . . . Well, I gotta gallop once around." She waved to Trish. "See ya."

By the end of morning works, Trish had ridden her own three, Diego's one, and three for Adam. Gatesby had given her a real ride—even her arms felt sore.

"How's it feel to be back in harness?" Adam asked as they headed for the track kitchen.

"Sore." Trish rubbed her right shoulder. A gift from Gatesby.

"A love bite?" David tapped her on the same spot.

"Owww." Trish flinched away. "Knock it off, David."

Patrick held the door open for all of them.

After breakfast David and Patrick prepared to head back.

"Did you call Mom last night?" David asked Trish.

"No, I thought you were going to."

David glared at her. "You said you'd call. I heard you tell Mom you would. You'd better start taking some responsibility."

Stung by her brother's criticism, Trish felt hurt. She'd have to do better, she knew that. They walked to where they'd parked the silver-and-blue van the night before. "Drive safely now," Trish echoed her mother.

David swung up into the driver's seat. "You sound like Mom. Call her once in a while. She still worries even if she won't admit it."

"Yes, boss." Trish touched a finger to her forehead. She waved to Patrick. "You guys coming down for some of the races?"

"We'll see."

"Bring Mom . . ." Trish could hear a note of pleading in her voice. ". . . to the winner's circle."

David tooted the horn as he turned the van around and drove out the entrance toward Highway 101.

Trish felt like another part of her was being torn away—piece by piece. Soon there wouldn't be anything left of her. She kicked the gravel with the toe of her boot, and headed back to the barns. She'd wanted to come to California, and now she was here. What next?

Back at the condo she moved the rest of her things

into her room and got settled. The next afternoon, Martha insisted on driving Trish over to the nearby college to register for the chemistry class. She would have classes four evenings a week from six to nine. One of those nights was a lab.

Trish purchased her books in the bookstore and glanced through them on the way back to the Finleys'. "Yuck."

"Not your favorite class?"

"No. They let me drop it because of all the pressure of racing and training, and then my dad being sick. But I'll tell you, I wasn't getting it. David tried tutoring me, but I just don't like chemistry."

"Why are you taking it?"

"I promised my mom. It's one of the requirements for college." Trish shut the book and slipped it back into the plastic bag. "You know any good tutors?"

"Check with your teacher the night of your first class. Maybe he or she will know of a student from last semester."

Trish nodded. "Good idea. Thanks."

———

Class started the following Monday, and Trish found a tutor right away. Finding a regular time to meet wasn't as easy. They finally settled on Saturday night, because Bay Meadows had late racing on Fridays.

Training was hard enough, and then racing would begin. There were the morning works, time for meals, afternoon study, and classes in the evenings. Then it was to bed and up again to start over.

Trish's agent, Henry Garcia, met her at the kitchen

on the morning of opening day. "I have two mounts for you."

"Okay."

"Second and fourth. You need to be in the jockey room by noon." He went on to tell her about the trainers and the horses. "I have only one for you tomorrow, in the seventh."

Trish waited for the thrill of excitement to bubble up. There was nothing there. "Thanks," she managed. After draining her orange juice glass, she took her tray back to the window.

At the barn she was met by two people. One of them sported an expensive camera. She could recognize reporters a mile away by now.

"You have a couple of minutes?" The young woman swept a strand of long, dark hair behind her ear and offered her hand. "I'm Amanda Sutherlin from *San Mateo Express*, and this is Greg Barton, our photographer."

"Hi." Trish shook his hand too. "I'm in a bit of a hurry. What can I do for you?"

Amanda dug a notebook out of a cavernous black bag. "Just a few questions, if you don't mind."

Trish nodded.

"What brought you to Bay Meadows?"

"Adam Finley. He insisted this would be a good place for me this summer."

"Couldn't you race anywhere in the country after winning the Triple Crown?"

"Possibly. But we've had some personal problems."

"I know. I'm sorry." Amanda glanced down at her notes. "How has that . . . your father's death . . . affected your riding?"

"It hasn't, as far as I know." Trish looked around to

see Adam standing beside her.

"Did you bring horses down here to race?"

All the usual questions were asked, and Trish answered as best she could, backed up by Adam. She wasn't sure which was better—to talk about her father, or not. Pastor Mort had said talking about him would make it easier. But it seemed as if it made everyone uncomfortable, and brought back the pain.

Trish mulled the question over in her mind on the way to the jockey dressing rooms near the grandstands. Tall palm trees enhanced the visitor's entrance to the track, but offered little shade. Buses were already delivering loads of senior citizens. The stands were filling up for opening-day ceremonies.

Trish settled into a chair with her chemistry book and notebook. So far she was keeping up, but much of what they'd covered she'd already had. Reviewing it made her realize how quickly she forgot the stuff.

She chewed on a pencil while working out the equations. The women's jockey room, while clean and freshly painted, had none of the amenities of the men's. And none of the bustle. Two other female jockeys sat talking in a corner. They'd greeted Trish when they came in and then left her to her homework.

When the second race was called, Trish put her books away and began her pre-race routine. She polished her boots, cleaned and waxed her layers of goggles. At least a dry track surface meant no mud. She did her normal stretching, and finally put on green silks with a yellow diamond pattern. She snapped the cover over her helmet and waited for the call to the weighing room.

When she stepped outside to walk to the scale, her butterflies came alive and flipped a couple of aerial loops and spins.

"One-o-one." The man running the scale intoned, then grinned at her. "Welcome to Bay Meadows, Trish. And good luck."

Back to the weight training, Trish thought, realizing she'd lost four pounds. She knew most of it was muscle. Where would she find the time to work out in the schedule she'd set for herself?

She followed the parade of jockeys through the side entrance of the grandstands and into the saddling paddock. The stands were full and spectators lined both sides of the walkway. It almost felt like home.

Restless feet and a slashing tail told Trish that her mount in position six was unhappy about something. The tall, rangy dark bay rolled his eyes when she entered the stall.

"This is his first out since he got cut up in a fall last winter," the trainer said. "Take him to the outside where he can run without being bumped around."

Trish nodded and lifted her knee for the mount. The horse laid his ears back when he felt her weight in the saddle.

He fought her all the way to the starting gates. It took three tries to get him in. Trish tried to settle him down and get him thinking about racing, but when the gates flew open he hung back. They were already a stride behind when he finally lunged through the gate.

Trish swung him to the outside, and by the end of the first turn had the gelding running like he should. The field ran six lengths ahead of them. She went to the whip and brought him even with the next runner, then moved him up as they rounded the next curve. But no matter how much she used the whip, he quit on her down the stretch. They finished dead last.

The next race wasn't much better. They finished off the pace by four.

"Tough luck," Adam consoled Trish that night when she returned from her chemistry class.

"Yeah. I just couldn't get them to run. I don't know, I didn't—" She paused, trying to put words to her feelings. "I just didn't seem to communicate with them; not like usual."

She went to bed that night feeling depressed. Where had the fun of racing gone?

CHAPTER 13

Trish was boxed in again. She felt like screaming in frustration. Gatesby had broken well from the gate, but here they were on the final turn and she had no where to go. If she dropped back they'd be clipped by the horses behind.

Finally the horse on the outside dropped off the pace. Gatesby burst through the hole, but it was too late. They finished fourth.

"Sorry. That was hard to take," Adam commiserated as they walked the gelding back to the barns.

"I shouldn't have let it happen. I must have been asleep or something." Trish slapped her whip against her boot. "Good thing Anderson didn't come all the way from Portland to watch his horse." She patted the gelding's steamy neck. "You deserved better than that, fella."

"Well, you can't beat yourself up over it. Things will turn around. You're too good a jockey for them not to."

"I'm beginning to wonder."

That evening there was a letter from Red. Trish still hadn't answered the last two. She slumped down on the sofa so she could enjoy the night lights while she read. He'd won again. *Glad someone is winning.* And he missed her. She stared out the window, thinking, *Do I really miss him?* If you missed someone weren't they in your thoughts—at least part of the time? Her thoughts seemed to be in a turmoil. Or was she thinking at all?

She toyed with the idea as she climbed the stairs to her room. She found a note on her bed from Martha. *"Help yourself to whatever you'd like to eat. We've gone to a friend's for dinner."*

Trish smiled at the happy face drawn at the bottom of the page. If only she had more time to spend with Martha. They'd have to set a date and go out to lunch and do some shopping. Maybe get some school clothes.

She was too tired to go back downstairs for something to eat. Instead, she fell into bed and back to the blessed emptiness of sleep.

Trish only pulled a D on her first chemistry quiz. She felt as if she'd been kicked by a flying hoof. The rest of the lecture passed in a blur. *Throw if off*, she ordered herself. *You can't let this get you down.*

But it did. It was one more failure to pile on to a load that was getting too heavy to bear.

Her mount the next afternoon swung wide on the turns and finished fourth.

"If I could just have kept him running straight, we'd have been in the money." She slumped on a green wooden trunk in the office at the barns. "What is the matter with me?"

Adam looked up from his paperwork. "I think you're trying too hard. You talked about going home for a couple of days. Maybe you should; it might help."

"I'd have to cancel a ride on Sunday. . . . Big deal, the owner would probably be glad to give it to someone who wins once in a while. What about the one for you on Saturday?"

"I'll get someone; don't worry."

"If I skip my lab on Thursday . . ." She shook her head. "No. I'll catch an early flight on Friday morning. Maybe David can pound some chemistry into my head on Saturday. If he'll even talk to me, that is."

"Trouble there, too?" Adam leaned back in his green and gold director's chair.

"Yeah. I haven't been too faithful about writing and calling home."

You haven't been too faithful about anything, Nagger jumped in.

Adam handed her a phone book. "Call the airline now. It'll make you feel better."

———

Thursday afternoon, Trish rode Robert Diego's gelding to a place. They missed the win by a photo finish.

"You can't complain about that," Adam said as he snapped a lead shank on the gray's halter. "You rode well and that was a tough field. Any horse could have been the winner."

"I shoulda gone to the whip sooner. He could have done it."

"Trish . . ."

"Well, I won with him before."

"That was Portland. The horses here are faster. He did very well."

Trish planned to study the next morning on the plane, but fell asleep. It was easier.

Trish saw Rhonda's beaming face before she saw her mother's as she walked up the ramp from the plane. From the looks of it, Rhonda was in her perpetual-motion mode. She threw her arms around Trish, backed off, then hugged her again.

"Wow! Look at your tan. You been laying out or what?"

"Just the arms and face. The rest of me's white as ever. I don't have any daylight hours to lay out, even though there's a deck right off my bedroom. I've only been on it once."

"My turn," Marge laughed as she reached in for a hug. "I can tell I won't get a word in edgewise this trip home. You have other luggage?"

"Nope, this is it." Trish picked up her sports bag again. "I travel light when I can."

"And you're only staying till Monday," Rhonda groaned. "Why is it my best friend is always in some other part of the country?"

"That's the price of fame." Marge led the way down the escalator and back up to the parking lot.

Trish stopped on the sidewalk to look at Mt. Hood with its summer snow streaks. Mount St. Helens was just visible to the north. "No mountains in San Mateo. I feel like I'm really home."

"Maybe someday we'll go skiing again." Rhonda turned to Trish and grinned. "Then, maybe not. Wait till you see—"

Marge stopped at a black-cherry-colored mini-van and inserted her key in the lock. "What do you think?" She smiled at Trish.

"What a beauty! You didn't tell me you bought a new car."

"I wanted to surprise you." Marge flipped the electric lock and opened the passenger doors. "Just toss your stuff in. You two can fight for the front seat."

"What'd you do with the wagon?" Trish gave Rhonda a playful shove toward the front.

"I traded it in. Your father and I had looked at this one before, and our mechanic said the wagon needed work, so . . ." She slammed her door shut. "Here we are."

Trish felt the old familiar pain at the mention of her father. When she walked into the house, it hit her like a load of rock, and she could hardly make it to her bedroom.

"Still hurts, huh?" Rhonda sat down on the edge of the bed and hugged a throw pillow to her chest.

Trish nodded. "Shows, huh? It's not so bad when I'm away from home. But when I come back, and he's not here—" She went to look out the window, her hands stuffed in the back pockets of her jeans. "I don't know, Rhonda. Sometimes I wonder if the pain will ever go away."

"Wish I could help, Trish."

"I don't think anyone can." She stood at the window, silent for a few moments. "Let's go see Miss Tee."

Caesar met them at the door, tail thumping, and yipping with excitement.

"Where were you? You missed the car coming in. Some watchdog you are." Trish bent over to tug on his fluffy mane, and got a lightning-quick nose lick for her efforts. Then the dog put one white paw on Trish's knee to balance himself and pawed the air with the other. Trish pulled his ears and knelt down to hug him.

"No dogs at the Finleys' city home, though they have two Rottweilers on the ranch." Trish stopped to look over the farm. She could see the horses in their paddocks beyond the barns. Patrick's new mobile home looked settled in on the property. The base was covered with matching skirting, and there were newly planted shrubs and flowers to make it look homey.

The girls trotted on down the rise. Trish's whistle was answered by a whinny from the paddock. Old Dan'l hadn't forgotten her. But Spitfire's shrill response was as absent as Hal's voice.

Trish stopped in the tack room to grab a carrot out of the refrigerator, and broke it into pieces as she and Rhonda meandered past the stables and out the lane to the paddocks.

Miss Tee trotted up to the fence and stood still when Trish took hold of the halter. She munched her carrot and nosed Trish's hand for more. Double Diamond and his dam did the same.

"Where'd you learn those manners?" Trish rubbed the filly's ears and the crest of her mane. "You sure are getting to be a beauty."

"She always has been. Remember what a cutey she was when she'd peek around her mother with the mare's tail draped over her face?" Rhonda patted Double D. "This one's pretty good-looking, too."

Dan'l nickered from the next paddock. The yearling and two mares joined him at the fence. *If only Spitfire were here.* Trish leaned her forehead against the filly's.

"There'll never be another horse like Spitfire." She shook her head.

"You two had a pretty special relationship. I think he could read your mind and you his."

"I know. You know what scares me?" The filly blew in her ear.

"What?"

"I can't read my horses anymore. It's like we're not even on the same wavelength. You know how my dad used to say I had a special gift?" She closed her eyes. "It's gone."

"Oh, Trish, I . . ." Rhonda patted Trish's shoulder.

"If I can't race, I don't know what I'll do. Life just isn't worth it."

"Tricia Marie Evanston, don't talk like that!" Rhonda's temper flared like her red hair. "Things'll get better again. I know they will."

Double Diamond raced off at the sound of the raised voice. Miss Tee pulled against Trish's restraining hand. Trish let her go. "I hope so." She wandered over to pat Dan'l. "I sure hope so. It can't get any worse."

"Welcome home, lass," Patrick called as they returned to the barn. "What do you think of the home stock?"

"They're looking good, Patrick. And so are you. Your house is beautiful. You've been working hard."

"Well, your mother's done a lot of it. She sure has a green thumb. What's this I hear about you losing your touch?"

"It's true. I can't bring in a winner for the life of me." Trish and Rhonda flopped on a hay bale in front of the tack room.

"And she says life isn't worth living."

"Blabbermouth." Trish elbowed her friend in the ribs.

"It'll get better, lass, it will." Patrick propped a leg on another bale and leaned his elbow on his knee. "What's that saying?" He wrinkled his brow. "It's always darkest before dawn?"

"Yeah, well dawn better come pretty soon." Trish levered herself to her feet. "You need me in the morning?"

"Nope. You're on vacation; sleep in."

David was about as friendly as a porcupine at the dinner table that night. He only answered when spoken to.

"What's with him?" Trish questioned her mother as she helped clear the table.

"Why don't you ask him?" Marge rinsed plates in the sink and loaded them into the dishwasher.

The thought of getting into an argument with David was more than Trish could handle. So much for having a chemistry coach.

Her mother had turned down the sheets, and Trish's bed welcomed her. She watched the dancing tree branches make shadows on her wall before sleep claimed her.

"Okay, David, what is it?" she asked after breakfast the next morning.

David looked up from circling the rim of his coffee mug with a forefinger. "You really want to know?"

Trish nodded.

"Okay. You don't call. You don't write. If Mom didn't talk with Martha, we wouldn't know if you were dead or alive." David set his mug down hard. "Even Red's called here asking if you're all right. What are we supposed to tell him?"

Trish's sigh could be felt all the way to her toes. "I'm sorry." She sucked in her bottom lip. "What can I say? You're right."

"I hear Mom crying at night. Losing Dad was bad enough; she shouldn't have to cry about you too."

A gray cloud settled around Trish's shoulders and pressed her to her chair. "I'll do better. I promise."

David stared at her. "Is that all you've got to say?"

Trish nodded.

"I expected you to at least yell at me." A tiny grin lifted one corner of his mouth. "I had all kinds of answers ready."

Trish was speechless. She could hear her mother talking to Caesar out on the deck.

"The four musketeers are going for pizza and a movie this afternoon. How does that sound?"

Trish looked at her brother for the first time in a long time—really looked at him. The frown was gone from his forehead. Her brother, her friend, was back.

———

That afternoon at the Pizza Shack, Brad asked David, "When do you leave for Arizona?"

"First week in September. I've been accepted and all my records are transferred."

"That was fast."

"How come I . . ." Trish shut her mouth. If she'd called home more often, she'd have known.

"I can't wait. I'll have a year-round tan then, not just rusty like you Washingtonians."

"Yeah, big talk." Rhonda flicked soda at him with her straw. "You know for sure where you're going to school, Brad?"

"Mom says Clark, Dad says University of Washington, and my scholarship is for Washington State. I had thought David was going to be there and we could room together." He rested his chin on his hands. "I'm accepted at all three."

"Now the *big* question. What are you going to be when you grow up?" Rhonda teased.

Trish felt like a spectator watching a play from the last row of the balcony. The voices faded in and out, as with a faulty sound system.

"What are you going to do, Tee?"

Trish snapped to attention. "Who, me? Uh—join the

foreign legion." Trish took a bite of pizza before looking up to get her friends' response.

"Funny." David shook his head.

"We're seniors this year." Rhonda jumped in to fill the silence. "We can do anything we want."

"Right." David and Brad spoke in the same breath.

Trish sat through the movie but couldn't have told anyone the plot. Rhonda stayed overnight with Trish, and though they usually didn't lack for things to talk about, Trish had to force herself to stay awake. She drifted off in the middle of a sentence.

In the morning, Marge insisted they all go to church together. Trish felt about as much like going to church as to the dentist. She was the last one out to the mini-van, and sat in the back. Rhonda turned to talk with her but Trish was not in the mood.

She managed to ignore the songs, the Scripture-reading, and the sermon, until Pastor Mort quoted Jesus: "In my Father's house are many mansions . . . I go to prepare a place for you, that where I am you may be also."

Trish clamped her teeth on her bottom lip. Her father had quoted that verse many times. She glared at the pastor. Had he purposely used this scripture—because he knew she would be there? Arms locked across her chest, Trish mulled the thought over, trying to put his voice in another dimension.

Rhonda poked her in the side. "You okay?" she whispered.

Trish shook her head.

The service closed with the hymn from Isaiah: "He will raise you up on eagle's wings . . ." Trish tried to shut it out. When that didn't work, she walked out the door. It may have been her theme song at one time, but not anymore.

"Pastor Mort asked about you," Marge said when she got to the car. "He wondered why you left suddenly. Do you want to go back in and say hello? We'll wait."

Patrick nodded. "It might do you good, lass."

Trish erupted from the backseat. "How come everyone knows what's best for *me*?" Her voice broke as she climbed out of the van and slammed the door after her.

She met Pastor Mort as he was entering his study. "I—I'm sorry I left church like that. I just couldn't take any more." She slouched in a chair in his office.

"I thought so. You looked pretty uncomfortable." His smile was easy; his voice without condemnation. "Contrary to what you might have thought, I did *not* choose that scripture passage. It was the assigned portion for today."

Trish had to grin. He'd read her perfectly.

"I know that was one of your father's favorite verses. He was looking forward to that mansion, you know." Pastor Mort waited for Trish to say something. He was good at waiting.

"I didn't want to come to church today—"

"I figured as much. How's the anger these days?"

Trish grinned again. "Better, I think. It's hard coming home, though. Everything comes back as soon as I walk in the door." She looked down at her hands. "I can't do anything right anymore, either. I can't ride like I used to; can't win anything. And I nearly flunked my chemistry quiz—and I'd studied. All I want to do is *sleep*. I can't breathe; it's like the air is too heavy."

Pastor Mort nodded. "Depression can be a part of the grieving process. It happens when we turn our anger inward. Does that seem to fit?"

"Maybe."

"Have you read your father's journal?"

Trish shook her head.

"Have you started one of your own?"

"I—I just don't have time right now. I—" She looked up to study the man's face. "I'm scared. Really scared."

"Why is that?" His voice was soft, compassionate.

Trish sensed that he really cared. "I—I don't think life is worth living anymore."

"Too much effort?"

"Mmmm."

"May I pray with you, Trish?"

Trish shook her head.

"Well, if I can't pray with you now, I promise I will pray *for* you."

She nodded, holding back the tears.

"Try the journaling. I know it will help. I could find someone down there for you to talk to, if you'd like."

"I gotta go. They're waiting for me." Trish stood to her feet. "Thanks."

"It'll get better. Believe me." Pastor Mort stood with her. "I'll send you the name of someone in San Mateo."

———

The next morning Marge drove Trish to the airport. "What did you think of Miss Tee, Trish?"

"Patrick's been doing a good job with her."

"No . . . I have."

Trish stared at her mother. "You?"

"Yes. Surprised?"

"Surprised isn't the word; you don't even *like* horses."

Marge drove into the short-term parking lot and turned off the engine. "It's funny, isn't it. All the years your father worked with the horses, I was busy raising you kids. Now he's gone, and you and David . . ."

"But I'm coming back."

"I know that. But you'll start your senior year this fall. After graduation who knows where you'll be." Marge turned toward her daughter. "I needed something to do—something to really occupy my time—so I asked Patrick if I could help with the horses. It's been good. I feel closer to your dad down at the barns than anywhere. Maybe it's because he was so happy there." She continued as the tears ran down her cheeks. "I found that I'm good with the babies. Of course, I always have been good with babies . . ."

"Oh, Mom, I'm really proud of you."

"Thanks, Tee. I figured it couldn't hurt to try. Selling out had crossed my mind. How are things going for you in California?"

It was the first chance all weekend that Trish had had to really talk to her mother. "Not too good. I've lost my touch—can't seem to get them into the money."

"I'm sorry to hear that." Marge laid a hand on Trish's shoulder.

"The sportswriters even talk about it in their articles. Pretty bad, huh?" She opened the car door. "We'd better go."

"I know . . . Just remember that I love you—and miss you. The house is pretty empty."

Trish tried to smile around the quiver of her lips. "It won't be too long till I'm home."

Aboard the plane, Trish pondered her mother's words—"selling out." Would her mother ever really consider that? Was there anything she could do to stop it?

The next afternoon, Trish's mount stumbled coming out of the gate. The filly went to her knees, and Trish somersaulted over her head and thumped in the dirt.

CHAPTER 14

Trish took the roll on her shoulder.

Her mount lunged back up on her feet and galloped down the track after the receding field.

Trish continued the somersault roll to a sitting position and took a moment to get her bearings. She sat in the dirt of the track, breathing hard; coughing, and spitting some dirt from her mouth. After flexing her arms and legs to be sure everything was intact, she staggered to her feet, still a bit woozy from the force of the fall.

A track ambulance stopped beside her and the paramedics jumped out. "You okay?" one asked as he swung open the rear door and reached for his case.

"I'm fine. You don't need any of that stuff." Trish flinched when she moved her head. "I'm just shook-up." She grimaced again when she touched her right shoulder.

"Bruised too, I'd guess." A young woman grasped Trish's right hand. "Squeeze." She watched Trish's flinching response. "You'd better have them look at that in First-Aid. Come on, jump in. We'll take you over there."

Jumping was a bit beyond Trish's ability at that moment, but she climbed into the ambulance for the ride to the nurse's station in the same building as the jockey rooms.

By the time Trish sat down on a gurney in one of the curtained-off examining alcoves, her shoulder was throbbing. She rotated it carefully. It worked, but it hurt.

Waiting for the nurse, Trish laid back and closed her eyes.

"I think she's done for as far as racing is concerned." Trish tried to ignore the man's voice on the other side of the room, but he spoke too clearly. "Anyone could have won on Spitfire; he was that good."

"I don't know," the other voice responded. "She's won plenty of other races too."

"Yeah, *before* her father died. She's just a lucky kid who's run out of luck." His voice was a hoarse whisper, but Trish heard him with no trouble.

Does he think I'm deaf or something?

"No better than a green apprentice. It was all hype, nothing more."

Was it true? Is that what people were actually saying and thinking about her?

"So, how're you doing?" A gray-haired nurse with a warm smile swished back the curtain. "Heard you took quite a spill out there."

Trish nodded. "It's just my shoulder. A hot shower'll take care of the rest." The man's insensitive words pounded in her brain. While the nurse helped her remove her silks, she could feel the anger and hurt burning in her stomach and flaring up into her chest.

Trish winced when the woman moved the injured shoulder and gently but firmly felt for a break. "Just a bruise, I'm sure. You have any more mounts today?" Trish shook her head. "Good. Let's ice it and put it in a sling to take the pressure off. Knowing jockeys, though, you'll be up and riding again tomorrow."

Trish tried to smile, but it felt as if her face would crack with the effort. Was her gift with horses really gone? Buried with her father?

The nurse slapped a chemical ice bag to activate it. Trish turned onto her stomach, and the woman placed the bag high on Trish's shoulder blade, then pulled a sheet over her.

"Lie there with the ice for a bit, and I'll get you some aspirin. A nap wouldn't hurt either."

But sleep was out of the question. Trish had a hard time lying still. When she squirmed, the pack slipped. She slid it back in place again and took a deep breath to relax. The pack slipped again. Trish rolled over and swung her feet to the floor. *This is not working.*

She pulled her silk shirt around her shoulders and headed for the door. In the hall she ran into the nurse. She shook her head. "Why don't you go down to the whirlpool and then see the masseuse?"

"Yeah, thanks."

"And use the sling . . ."

Trish ignored the pain in her shoulder as she changed clothes in the women's jockey room. She jammed her things into her sports bag, her arm back in the sling, and hurried out the door. All the way around the south end of the track and into the parking lot, her shoulder throbbed and the anger churned in her stomach.

Slinging her bag in the backseat of her car, Trish slid into the driver's seat. She punched the button to put the top down and started her engine.

Each time she shifted, the pain in her arm reminded her of the pain in her heart, the pain in her mind. *How much more of this can I take?*

She stopped for the lights, northbound on Camino

Real. She had no particular destination. The sign read "92 to Half Moon Bay." Trish took the cloverleaf and headed west, over the hills to the Pacific Ocean.

The winding road invoked speed. Trish shifted down on the upgrade and leaned on the accelerator. Wind blew her hair back and made her eyes water. She roared around one curve and hit the brakes. A truck and trailer rumbled up the grade in front of her.

You don't learn too fast, do you, her nagging voice shouted above the roar of the car's engine.

Trish backed off. All she needed right now was a traffic ticket or, worse, an accident. The truck picked up speed after it crested the last hill. Trish could see the ocean in the distance. She followed the curving road down between bushy hills that finally opened onto a narrow valley, lined on both sides with Christmas tree farms. As the valley widened, she passed truck farming, a winery, and the houses and businesses of the town of Half Moon Bay. The road ended at a traffic light on Highway 1.

Waiting for the light, Trish debated. Left or right—where was the nearest beach? Because she was in the left-hand lane, she turned south when the light changed. She watched for beach access signs, but only saw more housing and planted fields of squash or pumpkin that reminded her of her mother's garden. There were huge green spiky plants that looked like thistles along the sides of the road.

Finally, she spotted a sign—"Redondo Beach." It pointed to the right. She turned at the edge of a golf course and slowly followed a bumpy road between giant eucalyptus trees. She'd asked Adam about them one day.

Today's heat caused their pungent aroma to drift on the breeze.

A poor excuse for a fence corralled a group of horses to her left. It was made of sticks, baling wire, bent or broken posts, and colored baling twine. Her father would have deplored a fence like that.

The road dead-ended in a parking area on a high bluff. Trish could see a beach off to the right and a few small buildings. To the left a sign read "Strawberry Farm." There was a house with lots of windows over-looking the ocean. She got out of her car and shaded her eyes to look over the water. A freighter steamed north on the horizon. A couple of small fishing crafts bobbed on the swells closer in.

The surf roared below, while gulls rode the thermals and screeched overhead. *A peaceful scene*, Trish thought. *Where's the peace?* She reached for her bag in the back-seat. Stuffing it into the trunk, Trish grabbed a blanket that was kept there for occasions such as this. When she pulled it out, she saw a box she didn't remember bring-ing.

She dropped the blanket and picked up the box. An envelope was taped to the top of it. There was a note inside, in her mother's handwriting.

Dear Trish,
I hope you find this when you need it and are ready for it.

Love always, Mom.

Trish's fingers trembled as she cut the tape that se-cured the lid with her car keys. She took a deep breath. *Do I really want to see what's in this box?*

She shook her head at the silly thought. What could

possibly be in a box from her mother that she wouldn't want to see?

She lifted out the first item, wrapped in newspaper. "No!" She knew by the weight of it that she held the carved eagle she'd given her father for Christmas. Gently undoing the paper, she ran her hand along the delicately carved wings, then set it down, her jaw clenched against the memories. There were three books in the box also. On top was her father's journal, then the blank book he'd given her to write in, and finally, her own Bible.

Trish rubbed her aching shoulder and stared at the contents of the box as if they were a snake ready to strike.

She could hear Pastor Mort's voice in her head: *"Read your father's journal."*

"No. I can't handle this right now." She slammed the trunk lid shut and started down the steep embankment to the beach. A third of the way down, Trish stopped short. She'd forgotten her blanket.

She turned and wearily climbed back up the washed-out path. When she opened the trunk for the blanket, she impulsively grabbed the two journals with it and slammed the lid again.

After slipping and sliding her way to the hot sand, she walked up the beach a ways before dropping her stuff at the base of the cliff. She took off her tennis shoes and socks, rolled up the pant legs of her jeans, then jogged down to the surf.

"Yikes! I thought California water was warm." She backed up and let a dying wave wash over her feet. The backwash sucked the sand out from under her heels. As her feet adjusted to the frigid water, she followed the wave action out, tugging on her pants in an effort to keep them dry. When a wave slapped higher than she thought it would, she threw up her hands and waded farther. Next time she'd bring shorts and a swimsuit.

But even the crashing symphony of the surf couldn't drown out the conflicting voices in Trish's head. She rubbed her burning eyes, and pounded up the beach at the edge of the waves. It didn't help. Nothing helped.

Trish returned to the blanket and flipped it out. The journals tumbled into the sand. She picked up her father's journal and carefully brushed it off. A pen dropped loose when she opened the clasp.

She flopped back on the blanket and shielded her eyes with her arm. *Do I really want to read this?* She sat up again and opened the book to the first page.

> *Dear God . . . Right now I am so angry I can't even begin to describe it. Why are you doing this to me? Cancer!* *I thought you loved me, and now this. How can this be consistent with love?*

Trish closed her eyes and rested her forehead on her bent knees. *He felt the same way I do!* She continued reading.

> *How can I love you and tell others about your love when you do this to me? Why didn't you just strike me dead and get it over with? Oh, God, why? Why?*

Trish wanted to shout the same questions, but with the lump in her throat she could hardly whisper. "Why did you take my dad away? He was a good man." She sobbed as she dropped the journal beside her on the blanket. "Why?"

A seagull drifted overhead, screaming into the wind.

Trish searched the blanket for the pen. She picked up the blank journal and began to write. The words flowed out as fast as she could get them down. There was no "Dear God," only hurt and rage and despair.

After a while her hand cramped and her eyes burned. Her throat was so dry she could hardly swallow. The sun hovered over a bank of gray fog that shrouded the horizon, and a breeze whipped sand over the edge of the blanket. Trish shivered. She flipped back to the first pages again. *I wrote that?* She wanted to rip out the pages, but caught herself. She dropped the book and picked up her father's again.

> *But I know God is my strength and power. He makes my way perfect. That is my Bible promise for today. I will hang onto it. How will I get through this without you, my Father?*

Trish slammed the book shut. She picked up her blanket and tucked the books into the folds. She had a chemistry class tonight.

Back in the car Trish slumped against the seat. She felt like a deflated balloon, but somehow rested too. She stared out at the fog creeping in to the shore, and watched a gull wheel and cry. He rose higher, then lower, basking in the flow of the wind current. Trish wished she could take life's ups and downs that effortlessly.

CHAPTER 15

When would she learn to study the right stuff?

Trish stared at the chemistry paper she'd just corrected. She'd missed four out of twelve this time—barely passing. Why was she wasting her time taking this stupid class? It wasn't as if she wanted to be a scientist or something. She bit down on her lip. Nothing was going right.

When Trish walked through the doorway to the Finleys' living room, she saw Martha reading in a chair by the window. The soft light seemed to surround her in a golden glow. A nature tape was playing, and the music was unbelievably peaceful. Martha looked up and smiled. "I'm glad you're home. How about something to eat?"

Trish dropped her bags on the stair. "I had some yogurt before class. I think I'm okay."

Martha rose to her feet. "Well, I'm hungry. How about a piece of homemade apple pie with ice cream? Adam says my pies would take a blue ribbon. I don't know about that, but I think they're pretty good."

"Okay." Trish felt lethargic. Maybe something to eat would help. She followed her hostess into the bright blue-and-white tiled kitchen. "All right if I have some milk with it?"

"Of course, dear. Help yourself. I'll have coffee." Martha set two plates on the glass-topped table in the bay window, overlooking a flower-bordered patio.

"Hmmm, this *is* good," Trish said, tasting the pie. "You bake as good as my mom."

"That's some compliment; I've tasted her baking. Marge gave me her recipe for cinnamon rolls. I'll have to make them while you're here."

When they'd finished eating, Martha asked, "What's happened, Trish? You look unhappy."

Trish tried to brighten up. "Oh, nothing."

"You can't fool me, Trish. Something is wrong. You'll feel better if you tell me what's troubling you."

Trish sighed. "I—I barely passed another chemistry quiz." She rubbed her shoulder. "Did Adam tell you I took a dive at the track?"

Martha nodded. "Yes. When you didn't return to the barns, he said he checked First-Aid. The nurse said you'd left in a hurry."

"I drove out to Redondo Beach."

"Oh? How bad is your shoulder?"

"It's just a bruise. I'm supposed to be wearing a sling, actually."

"Where is it?"

"In the car. I couldn't shift gears with it on."

"Trish, if I can help you in any way, I'd be grateful to do that. I know you miss your dad terribly, and you never talk about him. Someone told me something a long time ago that has stuck with me. 'A joy shared is doubled; a burden shared is cut in half.' Please let us help you."

Trish nodded. "Thanks. You always do." She shoved her chair back and picked up her plate and glass. "You know anything about chemistry?"

"I wish I did." Martha followed Trish to the sink. "Leave these till morning. How about if you and I go shopping Monday afternoon? I know you're needing school clothes, and I haven't shopped for something like that for years."

Trish looked at her in amazement. "I was going to ask you to go."

"See? Great minds . . ." Martha flipped off the light switch. "Hope tomorrow is better for you."

————————

Martha's good wishes seemed to help. Morning works went better than usual. Sarah's Pride acted as if she finally believed Trish was in charge, and Gatesby slow-galloped without pounding her to pieces. By the time they were finished with the entire string, Trish caught herself whistling. It was a tune she'd heard someone else singing on the way to the track.

She still felt great when she joined Adam in the saddling paddock for the second race. She stroked Firefly's neck and smoothed the filly's forelock. "How about your first race in California? You ready to whip 'em?" The filly rubbed her forehead against Trish's chest.

"You know, I'd rather you come from behind," Adam was saying. "Hang off the pace about third or fourth until the stretch. She's got plenty of power. Make sure you don't get boxed in on the rail. That happens real easy in the number-two position."

Trish nodded. Maybe this would be her day. Maybe she'd finally find herself in the winner's circle.

A good crowd filled the stands for the mile-long Camino Real Derby. The big purse had drawn some horses up from southern California. The parade to post increased Trish's feelings of both exhilaration and confidence. She patted the filly's neck.

"This is our day, girl; I can feel it."

Firefly stood quietly in the gate while the horses on both sides of her acted up. Number three had to be released and brought back in. At the bell, they broke clean. Firefly hit her stride immediately. So did the two on either side of her. Going into the first turn, the three were neck and neck. Halfway through the turn the horse on the outside bumped Firefly, who bumped the inside horse and sent it crashing into the rail.

Firefly kept her feet but lost ground. She straightened out on the stretch but couldn't seem to gain what she needed to be in competition. They finished fifth.

When Trish jumped to the ground, she saw blood running down the filly's rear leg. She'd been cut in the fray.

"That crazy jock on three," she muttered as she stroked the filly's neck. "He should be disqualified for riding carelessly like that. You're going to lodge a complaint, aren't you?" she asked Adam as soon as he'd inspected the wound.

"Yes, but it probably won't do much good. Three came in third."

"How bad is she?"

"I'll call the vet, just in case." Adam handed Trish her saddle. "See you back at the barn?"

Trish nodded. "If I'd just . . ."

"Trish, it wasn't your fault. You can't take responsibility for what every rider does." Firefly limped off behind him.

Trish didn't need Nagger. She scolded herself all the way to the barn, her anger rising with every negative thought. *Maybe everyone's right. Maybe I'm not any good anymore. I sure should have kept out of that mess. What a lousy ride.*

The vet had just finished checking Firefly's leg when Trish arrived. "How is she?"

"Not too bad. She's got plenty of heart to have finished with a cut like this. But it should heal clean." He turned to Adam. "Call me if there's any problem."

Trish went to the tack room and dug in the refrigerator for a carrot. Trish broke it in pieces and fed them to the filly one at a time, all the while telling her what a great horse she was. By sheer force of will, she kept her own anger at bay.

"See you tomorrow." She waved to Adam as she left the area.

"You okay?" he called.

Trish nodded and waved again. He couldn't see her tight jaw or burning eyes. She was not okay. Instead of going home, she took the road to Half Moon Bay.

Firefly was too good a horse to be messed up by an incompetent rider, Trish told herself. She kept up the internal harangue while swinging through the turns of Highway 92 to the ocean.

Arriving at Redondo Beach, Trish opened her trunk for her blanket and the journals. The box with the eagle inside had tipped over and the eagle was only partially wrapped. She pulled it out, securing it by the base. With one finger she followed the arch of the spread wing. She'd been so happy at the time to find the perfect gift for her father. Now he was gone—and his daughter couldn't even race anymore. *Why? . . . Why?*

Trish carelessly rewrapped the eagle and stuffed it into the box again, shoving the offending reminder as far back in the trunk as possible. She grabbed her books and blanket, a small cooler with drinks and an apple, and slipped and slid her way to the sand.

The sun played hide-and-seek between the high clouds as Trish hiked south from the trail. She threw her things on the sand, pulled off her shoes, and jogged to the water. The jog made her shoulder muscles scream with pain. The race, and the fact that she hadn't been wearing a sling hadn't aided its healing. Trish kicked at the foam frosting left on the beach by the outgoing tide. She wished she could run forever, leaving the hurt and pain behind her, but she tired quickly and trudged back to the blanket.

All of a sudden her anger flared against her father. Before he could break his smoking habit, he had developed lung cancer. *What kind of father would smoke, when he knew it could make him sick?* She opened her father's journal again, and the first words she saw were from the Bible. She slammed it shut.

I'm no good. I can't ride, let alone win, and I can't even get a decent grade on a stupid chemistry quiz. She lay back on the blanket, exhausted, wishing the sky would come crashing down on top of her.

After a while, she sat up again and stared out over the surf. Way out there her problems would be over . . . Trish rose to her feet and plodded to the edge of the water. A wave rolled in and rippled around her toes. She waded out to her knees.

I could just start swimming—straight out. Once through the surf, it would be so easy. She waded farther, oblivious to the depth. Waves broke and surged around her hips and waist. *Just keep on walking. Then start swimming. No more problems.*

Trish had no idea how long she stood watching the

horizon, transfixed. When a gull shrieked overhead, she realized her feet were so cold she couldn't move them.

She watched the gull. *To have wings like that . . . to soar and ride on the wind. To look down from that height. Maybe then I'd see all that was happening—and understand.*

"God, if you care at all, help me," she spoke aloud. "I can't stand this anymore."

Her feet ached, but she turned and forced one foot ahead of the other until she reached the shore and her things.

She crumpled to the blanket and wrapped it around her feet, rubbing them briskly.

When she picked up her journal, it fell open near the back. The pages were filled with handwriting. *What's this? I only wrote that junk to God in the front of the book.*

Trish looked again. It was her father's handwriting!

Dear Trish,

It was almost as if she could hear his voice.

If you are reading this, I'm either in the hospital near the end, or I'm with my heavenly Father.

No! her mind screamed. *I want you here with me—I need you!* Tears squeezed out from under her clenched eyelids. Then the dam burst. Great racking sobs shook her body. She hadn't cried liked this since her father's death.

I love you, Tee, with all my heart. I'm begging your forgiveness for my selfish habit that caused this whole thing. Knowing I must leave you and David and your mother breaks my heart. It's more than I can bear

alone. I wanted to see you grow up; see what a won-
derful young woman you would become. I wanted to
be there for you when you needed me.

Oh, Dad . . . God, please . . . She couldn't see for the
tears. She couldn't breathe for the sobs. She cried for all
the times she hadn't . . . couldn't . . . wouldn't.

I know that you are a fine and gifted jockey, Tee.
Don't let anyone convince you differently. Don't let the
hard times get you down. There will be some, you know.
Believe in yourself as I believe in you. And when you're
hurting, call on your heavenly Father. He hears you,
and He's there for you, no matter what happens. He is
the only one who can get you through the troubles of
life. He's gotten me through, even though I've failed
Him so many times.
"I know you will be angry. I know I was. But don't
become bitter, Trish. Tell God just how you feel. Let it
all out. You can't shock Him. He understands you and
knows you.
Always remember that I love you. I know where I'm
going . . . to the mansion He has prepared for me.
Someday, I'll meet you there, Trish. Don't ever give up.

Your dad

Trish lay back on the blanket, relief washing over her
like a wave. High above, a gull floated on the rising thermals. Then a song, almost audible, drifted on the wind
and echoed through the sandstone cliffs above her. "And
He will raise you up on eagle's wings . . . Bear you on the
breath of God . . ." The gull, dark against the sun, dipped
and soared. ". . . And hold you in the palm of His hand."
Trish hummed the familiar melody, allowing the
words to work their healing. The tears flowed again, unchecked, and a smile tugged at the corners of her mouth.

ACKNOWLEDGMENT

My thanks to Candy in the public relations department at Bay Meadows track in San Mateo, California, for the track tour and her wealth of information.